RIDERS OF THE BAR 10

After delivering a herd of prime longhorn cattle to the railhead town of McCoy, and being paid off in gold, Gene Adams and his crew headed back to Texas — a job well done. But soon they were ambushed and were lucky to escape with their lives. Worse still, they discovered their gold had been stolen somewhere along the trail. Gene and his men set off for a deadly showdown — with all the odds stacked against them.

Books by Michael D. George
in the Linford Western Library:

THE VALLEY OF DEATH
THE WAY STATION
DEATH ON THE DIXIE
KID PALOMINO

MICHAEL D. GEORGE

RIDERS OF THE BAR 10

Complete and Unabridged

LINFORD
Leicester

First published in Great Britain in 1999
under the name of 'Boyd Cassidy'

First Linford Edition
published 2001
by arrangement with
Robert Hale Limited
London

The moral right of the author
has been asserted

British Library CIP Data

George, Michael D.
  Riders of the Bar 10.—Large print ed.—
Linford western library
  1. Western stories
  2. Large type books
  I. Title
  823.9'14 [F]

ISBN 0–7089–4563–5

Published by
F. A. Thorpe (Publishing)
Anstey, Leicestershire

Set by Words & Graphics Ltd.
Anstey, Leicestershire
Printed and bound in Great Britain by
T. J. International Ltd., Padstow, Cornwall

This book is printed on acid-free paper

Dedicated to
Cowboys everywhere

1

The herd of longhorns was not as big as some that had headed to McCoy from the Bar 10 Ranch over the years. Yet, it was still larger than any other herd that had been brought out of Texas along the trail in over three dry summers.

Gene Adams led his men with the control that came from years of experience and grit. He had seen a lot of changes since he first drifted into the Lone Star state thirty years earlier and not all of them had been good. However, Adams was never one to allow the rose-tinted memories of his youth to blur his straight talking, straight thinking persona. He had lived long and hard by doing what he believed was correct. Time would prove whether he was right or wrong. Time would be his judge.

Gene Lon Adams was a man who sat

tall in his saddle as he rode in front of his herd of prime beef. His tanned face seemed to be that of a young man but his hair had long since bid farewell to any hint of colour and was as white as snow. None who ever knew the man felt that he was old yet they also felt that he had never truly been young. His was that rare breed of men. The sort who seemed always to have been wise and mature as if dropped from above into a saddle, fully grown. He had no true religion to hide behind as others often did, but he seemed able to understand the faiths of many and never took sides. Gene Adams was a man who never wronged anyone intentionally and would rather lose a fight than win by cheating. Not that he had lost many battles in his life. His was a rare purity of nature that had always believed in being square with folks.

Cheats get found out quick enough and tend to get shot at when they least expect it, he often told his men. He truly believed those words and all who encountered the silver-haired man came to believe them too.

He allowed his strong chestnut mare to drift along at her own steady pace as his men and his herd followed in his wake. Dust rose thick and true off the parched land over which the little-known trail wound through the prairie. Adams never used the trails of others and chose his own way at his own pace. Behind the herd stretched the vast spread that Adams had owned for half his life in the heart of Texas. The Bar 10 was huge, and profitable. It was said that it covered a million acres of prime grazing land, fringed by the mountains that kept the blue sky in its place. Gene Adams was said to have painted the sky blue when he first arrived in Texas because it matched his eyes.

Some men become legends.

Gene Lon Adams was such a man.

This was a herd of over five thousand head, all prime beef on the hoof and ready for market. They had filled their bellies on the thick sweet Bar 10 grass and were ready for the long drive when Adams had put the cattle drive together. Now they were within a day's steady walking of the McCoy railhead. There, Gene Adams would sell them for Yankee gold.

Apart from his two best friends, an old timer named Tomahawk and a youngster called Johnny Puma, the majority of the drovers were hired just for this trail drive. Gene Adams had left the remainder of his ranch hands back home on the Bar 10 tending to their chores and looking after the rest of his vast herd of longhorns.

Only the grizzly Tomahawk and youthful Johnny Puma were close to him, and always seemed to be at his side these days. Even Gene Adams needed friends he could trust along for the tedious back-breaking trail drives when he had so many strangers around him. These drovers whom Adams regularly hired made a living out of guiding other men's beef to market and were an unpredictable lot. Most were honest and often very quiet but there was always the odd wrong 'un who managed to get into the bunch however hard he tried to vet them beforehand.

This motley crew of cowboys had been the quietest Adams had used for several seasons but there were still a couple of them that he had doubts about. Tomahawk and Johnny Puma knew who these hands were and kept them under a watchful eye. In the past they had seen drovers disappear with dozens of their steers during drives to McCoy.

This had been a surprisingly uneventful cattle drive by anyone's standards but that meant nothing. They still had one night left before they finally reached McCoy, one night when trouble might raise its head. This was the one night when none of the three riders from the Bar 10 would sleep with both eyes closed.

Gene Adams was no stranger to gunplay and always packed his pair of gold-plated Colts in his gunbelt. The hand-crafted leather holsters had silver diamonds encrusted all over their black surfaces. Few made the mistake of pulling on him nowadays but there was always the odd fool in any pack. Adams had never killed anyone in all his years of adulthood although he had left a lot of men bleeding from having their gun hands blown apart by his speed and accuracy of aim.

Gene Adams was uneasy as he watched the sun getting lower above the distant mountain range ahead and spurred his mare on towards the awaiting chuck-wagon and the maniacal cook who was already preparing the evening meal.

Tomahawk was already there sitting with his back against a wagon wheel. This old man had been with Gene Adams since the early days and had never appeared anything else but old in all those years. Whatever his true age might have been was clearly nothing he ever thought about. Some are born old and Tomahawk was one of these. He had never revealed his real name to anyone except his boss and that was a place where secrets were safe. It was strange to see a white man with an Indian tomahawk tucked into his belt but this old man had one and was good with it. He could still throw it with lethal fury when required and hardly ever drew his forty-five. How he ever came to learn such an odd skill was another story and one that never was told the same way twice in succession. Tomahawk was a good man who looked up to the younger Gene Adams in a way that children respect their parents. He had acknowledged long ago that he was not as smart as his boss and, like a faithful hound, was happy knowing his place.

As Gene Adams dismounted and tied his mare to the long hitching rope that the cook had erected prior to starting the evening meal, he watched another rider approaching from the right flank of the nearby herd.

It was Johnny Puma on his pinto

pony. Puma had been with the Bar 10 for several years and had a reputation with his guns. Again he too hid behind a pseudonym. It was said that the man in his twenties had been an outlaw in his youth and only went straight after meeting up with the sobering figure of Adams. Whatever the truth behind this handsome young man's past it was again a secret known only to two men. Himself and the tight-lipped Adams.

Johnny Puma had a way of leaping from his pony long before the beast had quit galloping and somehow managing to stay upright on his Cuban heels. The pinto would continue to gallop for a few seconds before realizing that his master was no longer urging him on. Eventually the beast would turn and seek out the young man who fed and watered him, like a child seeking its mother.

Adams watched as the youngster jumped off the horse and ran up to the chuck-wagon. The smile on this young man's face was as broad as his shoulders.

'Grub ready, Gene?' he panted.

The cook gave a deadly glare at the trio of men as if warning them to stay away from his cast-iron pots as they sat amid the flames of the camp-fire.

'You tell that Joshua Jones critter to get the herd bedded for the night, Johnny?' Tomahawk asked from behind his whiskers as he stroked the sand beween his legs with a stick.

'I told him, our friend Mister Joshua Jones,' Johnny Puma replied as he pulled off his Stetson and beat the dust off it against the side of the wagon. 'He done spat a load of venom at me when I did.'

'Strange varmint that Jones,' Tomahawk sniffed.

'You can say that again,' Johnny agreed.

Gene Adams said nothing as he moved to the tailgate of the wagon and poured himself a cup of coffee. It was almost cold but it was wet. It washed the trail dust down and rested easy on his empty belly.

'You drinking that?' The cook asked as he carried on his duties around the trio.

'Yep,' Adams answered the strange man who never seemed to stop moving as he prepared the meals for the dozen men on the trail drive. 'Why?'

'Its cold, you dang fool.' The cook grabbed the pot and poured the remainder of the brown liquid away.

'Respect.' Adams pushed his tall ten-gallon hat off his face and smiled. 'This man has no respect.'

'Maybe you'll get some when I gets paid tomorrow.' The cook sniffed and emptied some grounds into the black pot before pouring a bucket of water on to them.

'Money ain't everything, cookie,' Tomahawk commented.

The cook sniffed again as he marched over to the roaring fire and rested the heavy pot on the hot coals next to the two stew pots. The smell that drifted from these vessels when the cook lifted off the heavy lids filled the three men's nostrils with the pleasure of anticipation. They were all damn hungry as they looked sheepishly at one another.

'Do you trust that Jones character, Gene?' Tomahawk asked, rubbing his bearded chin.

'He's a good hand,' Adams answered.

'Yep, but do you trust the critter?' Tomahawk repeated his question.

'I guess I only trust you and Johnny.' Adams removed one of his gloves and tucked it into his coat pocket. For some reason only known to himself he never removed his left-hand glove. Even the ancient Tomahawk had no idea why the elegant man hid his left hand from people's glares. There were tall stories that circulated around the camp-fires when Adams was out of earshot but it was all conjecture. This was a secret known to only one man and he was not about to satisfy anyone's idle curiosity.

Whatever the true reason for the

constantly gloved left hand, it certainly was not due to anything physical. Gene Adams could use that hand as well as his right.

He often drew his left gun rather than his right. It was a mystery that none had the grit to enquire about. Tomahawk had always figured that he would be told one day, if Adams wanted to tell him. That day had never come and probably never would but it mattered little to the crusty old-timer.

'What time will we get into McCoy tomorrow, Gene?' Johnny Puma asked as he sipped the cold water out of the huge ladle next to the water barrel.

'Around twelve, I guess.' The youngster smiled as his pinto returned to the other horses.

'Why you so happy, Johnny?' Tomahawk got to his feet slowly as he watched the young man grabbing his pony's reins and leading him to the hitching rope.

Adams turned with a knowledgeable expression etched upon his face. 'He's gonna get himself a girl, Tomahawk. He always gets himself a girl.'

'Dang fool,' the cook muttered as he raced past them with a tray of bicuits.

'That's the first thing you've said that I agree with, cookie.' Tomahawk grinned.

'The boy's young.' Adams chuckled. 'Remember how it was to be that young, old-timer?'

Tomahawk shrugged as he moved around the pair of men tending their horses. 'Remember what?'

'He was never young, Gene.' The broad smile of Johnny Puma flashed as he spoke.

'When Tomahawk was young,' Adams began, 'this range was covered in buffalo.'

Tomahawk gazed out at the flat prairie and nodded. 'Where did all them critters go, Gene?'

'I thought you shot them all, Tomahawk.'

For a moment the old man was

serious. 'Weren't me.'

Gene Adams tossed his saddle on to the ground and was still smiling as he noticed some of the drovers and wranglers heading in their direction.

2

Gene Adams was correct when he had said that they would reach the large cattle town of McCoy around noon. The church clock had just struck twelve times as the herd headed into Main Street. Five thousand head of prime beef tend to mess up streets pretty bad as they pass through but this was a well-managed herd that seemed almost too good as they headed for the vast acres of empty pens. This had been the best cattle drive that Adams had been on and he was giving silent thanks for his luck. Not even one stampede had slowed up their progress from the Bar 10 to McCoy.

Even with all the good fortune that had surrounded the long dry haul, Gene Adams was alert to the fact that after he had received his money for the longhorns and paid off his hands, his problems might only just be beginning. Gone was the threat of stampede or rustlers but now he had to get his gold back to the safety of the Bar 10.

As his men guided the seemingly endless lines of steers into the numerous cattle pens, Gene Adams watched with great interest at the dozen or more men perched high on the fence posts counting. It was only going to be a rough tally but he was happy to know that his job was done for another six months.

Adams turned his chestnut mare and rode towards the main office buildings that housed the buyers and shippers. He knew that timing was everything in getting a herd of steers to the rail-head in prime condition. The prices could change in a matter of days. He had seen times when he could barely get a dollar a head, yet on other occasions he was able to get over fifty per steer.

As he sat in his saddle he heard the distinctive sound of the black gelding that had been Tomahawk's pride and joy for the past two years.

'What's wrong, Gene?' the old man asked as he drew up alongside his boss.

'Just figuring,' Adams replied as he sat watching their reflections in the glass door-panes.

'Figuring what?'

'The final tally.' Adams took a deep breath and eased himself from the saddle. His foot found the sidewalk as he tied the reins tightly to the rail.

'Good job you knows your sums.' The old man smiled a smile that revealed few teeth and an awful lot of gum.

Gene Adams removed his right-hand glove and pushed it into his coat pocket as he stood trying to get the aches and pains out of his bones.

'What you want me to do?' the old man asked as he took a welcome swig from his canteen.

'Take the boys to the saloon and wait for me.' Adams removed his large hat revealing the red crease across his forehead as he did so. 'Better tell

Johnny to come over here and wait for me.'

'You expecting trouble, Gene?' Tomahawk looked anxious as he pulled his mount away from the rail.

'Nope,' Adams answered, 'but it don't pay to be foolhardy when you've got a lot of gold on you, does it?'

'I'll tell Johnny.'

Gene Adams watched as the old man rode his black horse towards the cattle pens where most of the drovers and wranglers were congregating. He entered the building with an air of a man who had done the same thing many times. He had. Only the amount of gold altered.

3

The saloon was busy as usual and the dozen or more men who entered with ten pounds of trail dust each upon their clothes did not raise one eyebrow amongst its regulars.

Tomahawk was, as always, the first to the bar and he tossed the silver dollars on to the counter top. His job was to keep the cowboys happy whilst Gene and Johnny got paid for the steers and then turned up to pay off the trail crew.

The men had big thirsts which had been getting bigger for over three long dry weeks on the trail. The drinks kept coming and the old man kept tossing the coins at the bartenders. He had his own bottle as usual and gently sipped the brown brew through the filter of hair upon his upper lip.

The saloon was filled with men of all sorts and descriptions from town drunks to sharp card-players. McCoy had them all in abundance like any other cattle centre. These were the vultures that hovered around the drinking holes trying to get a chance at taking a cowboy's hard-earned money off him before he had a chance to get back on the trail and ride home.

Tomahawk watched as the afternoon stretched out and the men got more and more the worse for wear. Empty bellies and cheap whiskey never mixed but it was a ritual that even the youngest drover had to experience. The old-timer knew that Gene Adams might have to wait for hours before everything was finalized and he got his gold. This was the time when the hands got very edgy. Some of the older men had been ripped off in the past and would start to impart their bad experiences of cattle bosses who would flee with their gold before paying off the hired help.

Tomahawk used every ounce of his experience to keep the cowboys relaxed and calm. His being there with them was the one factor that made the hands less worried. Everyone knew that the famous Gene Adams would never cheat anyone and, even more important, would never leave the old-timer behind. If Tomahawk was here, then Adams was nearby.

The gamblers began to multiply as the news of the cowboys got around town. They were gathering to try and skim some cream off these saddle-weary men. Big herds meant big crews and big money in small pockets.

Tomahawk had never seen so many white hats in one room before as the dudes practised their trade with each other waiting for the cowboys to get their wages. He had long since given up trying to advise wranglers not to play poker with men who could make cards appear or disappear into thin air. Now he just ensured that he kept them watered until Gene Adams showed up.

The clock above the wide warped mirror behind the bar struck two with a strange echoing sound as the two

21

horses pulled up outside. Tomahawk noticed the pinto pony and the chestnut mare before anyone else and walked towards the swing doors as his friends dismounted carrying two sets of hefty saddle-bags between them.

Gene Adams walked up the steps with one heavy set of bags over his left arm whilst Johnny Puma followed carrying the others over his broad shoulder. The enthusiastic welcome that the two men received from the cowboys resonated around the wooden building as Adams and Johnny made their way to a quiet corner and an empty table. The cowboys gathered around the pair as they sat down after placing the bulging bags on top of the stained wooden table.

One by one the hands were paid off in gold coins. Every man got a bonus which amounted to a doubling of their agreed wages. By the time Gene Adams had paid off the last drover, his bags were a lot lighter but still very full.

'What price did you get, Gene?'

Tomahawk asked from behind his dark bottle.

'Twenty-five dollars a head,' Adams answered.

'That good?' The old timer wondered aloud. Mathematics had never been his strongest point.

'After paying off the boys, I reckon we have made a pretty good profit for the Bar 10.' Adams secured the bags carfully as he noticed a tall man coming in their general dirction. He looked very mean and worse for wear. Tomahawk gave a quick glance over his shoulder and instinctively touched the Indian hatchet that protruded from his gun-belt.

'Trouble?' Johnny asked as he sipped at his beer, indicating the stranger.

'Could be.' Gene Adams stood carefully pushing his coat back over the handles of his golden Colts. 'Steady, boys. I'll try and handle this *hombre*.'

The old-timer slid out his tomahawk and gave his chair a nudge so that it faced the approaching man. He would act if he deemed it prudent. The weapon rested easily in his skilled hands.

The tall man seemed angry for some unknown reason and only stopped when he was within a few feet of the calm figure of Gene Adams. For a while their eyes burned into each other's souls as they stood almost toe to toe. Adams bore the dust of a long hard trail drive whilst this tall strange man appeared to have done little more than drink hard liquor for a long time.

'My name's Chargon.' The oily-skinned man said as if it should mean something to the three men. Only the young face of Johnny Puma seemed to react to the name as it touched a long forgotten memory buried deep within his brain. He held on to his cold beer and moved his weight in the chair where he sat as if balancing himself for action.

Gene Adams rubbed his thumbs over the hammers of his guns as he watched the tall man. 'Chargon?'

'Yep. You heard of me?'

'Nope.' Adams shrugged honestly.

'I have,' Johnny said in a low monotone. 'I heard about you a long time ago.'

Chargon seemed gratified by the recognition as he glanced hard into the young eyes of Johnny Puma. For an instant he seemed to recognize the youthful cowboy. 'We ever met, kid?'

'Maybe,' Johnny replied.

'What they call you?'

'This is Johnny Puma,' Gene Adams interrupted protectively.

Chargon shook his head. 'That weren't your handle when we last met, kid.'

Johnny Puma sat silently sipping his cool beer as he studied the man who seemed to have fallen a long way since his days of glory.

'Want something, Chargon?' Adams asked in a firm tone.

Chargon turned his attention back upon the mature solid figure of Adams who stood firmly before him. His eyes glanced at the two golden guns in their hand-tooled jewel-encrusted holsters, then at the saddle-bags on the table top.

'You seem to have a lot of money there, mister,' the man said, pointing at the saddle-bags. His voice was slightly slurred as he swallowed deeply.

'Correct, my friend.' Adams nodded. 'What concern is it of yours?'

'I ain't got enough money to get out of this damn town and you got all that,' snarled the stranger. 'Does that seem fair to you?'

'Depends on what you mean by fair, Chargon.' Gene Adams fixed his blue eyes on to the sunken pupils of the tall man.

The man had a gun hanging low on his hip from a holster that had long since been fit for its purpose. The leather stitching was loose and barely held the weight of the weapon. One might guess that Chargon had once been a very dangerous critter but now he was blurred by the consumption of very cheap whiskey; it was clear that the man did not realize what condition he or his tools were in. It was a rather sad sight to the silver-haired Adams.

'You are one of them Texas bastards, ain't you?' Chargon raised his hands until they became fists. Furious fists intent upon finding blood, Gene Adams's blood. The punch landed heavily on Adams's shoulder, sending him reeling backward a couple of steps. As the taller drunken man snarled and threw a second punch, Gene Adams raised his arms and absorbed the power of the blow on his elbows. Then, as quick as a flash, Gene used his strength to force Chargon back before letting rip with a right to the man's guts and a vicious left hook to his long unshaven chin. Chargon reeled on his heels and staggered for a few seconds before shaking his head. He gazed up at the silver-haired man, who was still within reach, as he wiped the blood from his mouth with his sleeve.

'Had enough?' Gene Adams asked coldly.

Chargon nodded. 'Yep. You win.'

'We've worked damn hard earning this for our ranch, my friend.' Adams slid his gloved hand into his coat pocket and pulled out a gold coin. He watched as Chargon focused upon it before he tossed it to him. Somehow Chargon's fumbling digits caught the coin. The tall oily man looked surprised at the sudden generosity from someone he had just been exchanging blows with.

'You get yourself a steak dinner, Mister Chargon,' Adams advised. 'You'll feel a lot better.'

Chargon was still glaring at the three men as he gripped the coin tightly. 'Reckon this will do for now.' He grinned.

'That's all you get from us,' Johnny Puma fumed over the top of his glass.

'I'll figure out who you really are, Mister Puma,' Chargon warned as he began to turn, spitting blood at the sawdust-covered floor. 'When I do, I'll come a'calling.'

Gene Adams held his gloved hand up

as if instructing his young friend to be quiet. He stepped closer to the man.

'Goodbye, friend,' Adams said through gritted teeth that seemed to regret his own generosity.

The man still seemed to be angry but backed off and moved towards the cowhands who were already starting to lose their hard-earned wages to the card tables. 'I'll be seeing you boys.'

Tomahawk rose to his feet and watched the angry man for a while before turning to his friends. 'That man is trouble with a gun.'

Gene Adams gave a quick look at the young figure of Johnny Puma who had sweat rolling down his cheek. He knew that the past had a way of catching up with even the fastest rider.

'Take it easy, Johnny,' he advised as the young man stood up next to him.

'We ought to get out of this town, boys,' Tomahawk said in an anxious voice as he carefully replaced his weapon back into his gunbelt. 'That varmint is crazy enough to use that coin to buy some bullets and come back spitting lead.'

Gene Adams patted his old friend on the shoulder. 'Get the horses tended and meet me and Johnny over at the stockpens in an hour.'

'We got time for some grub?' the old man asked as he aimed his boots at the saloon doorway.

'I ain't hungry,' Johnny sighed.

'Me neither,' Adams nodded.

★　★　★

The three riders rode their refreshed horses out of McCoy, leaving the trail hands enjoying themselves. Gene Adams led the trio as they retraced their route to the edge of the town and then turned off to a narrow trail. The men were heading along a route that Adams always took when he had a lot of gold in his saddle-bags. This trail was through a strip of woodland that gave them good cover.

The dangerous part of any trail drive

was getting safely home with the proceeds. Adams gripped his saddle horn tightly as they made their way through the tall parched trees.

They were hungry and had left McCoy quickly because they were vulnerable. Trouble was the one thing that money always attracted and the two saddle-bags tied to Johnny Puma's pinto and Gene Adams's chestnut were like time bombs. All three riders had a bad taste in their mouths as they rode away from the cattle town of McCoy.

Chargon had been drunk but he had also once been a pretty good hired gun and might just sober up long enough to get very ambitious. This thought drifted through each of the three riders' minds as they continued on along the remote trail.

'We better stop off at Sutters Corner,' Gene Adams shouted over his shoulder. 'We can stay the night there in the small hotel belonging to old man Davis.'

'We gonna eat his grub, Gene?'

Tomahawk grumbled.

'You got any better ideas?' Gene Adams turned his mare over a small crest and paused for a moment. In the distance he could see the rising of chimney-smoke. His two companions reined their horses to a stop beside him and looked through the hundreds of tall pines before them at the smoke.

'Old man Davis is an awful bad cook, Gene.' Tomahawk shook his head as he rested his arms upon his saddle horn.

'He's better than you with a skillet, old-timer,' Johnny smiled. It was the first time he had shown his teeth since being questioned by the strange figure of Chargon. It was as if he was finally beginning to relax and forget about the incident back at the rail-head township.

Gene Adams led the way through the maze of tall trees towards the distant chimney-smoke. 'Everybody cooks better than Tomahawk, Johnny.'

4

The gleaming gold coin in Chargon's grip seemed to drag the man from his self-pitying state of drunkenness, into a man who used the long bar mirror to study himself. What he saw, he did not like. Who was this wretch who forced his reflection back into Chargon's eyes? He refused the three fingers of whiskey that was placed before him by one of the bartenders and turned to watch the gathering of cowboys and gamblers. The saloon was buzzing with the electricity that easy money always brought to a cow town. He watched as the cards were dealt and played and the chips passed from one player to the next. He watched as the cowboys bought more and more chips with their trail wages and the gamblers smiled at one another as they expertly slid cards off the bottom of decks and somehow managed to let their victims beg to be taken. Chargon eased himself away from the wooden bar and ambled through the people until he was out in the street. The afternoon air felt good on his tired face as he stood gulping in the air that his lungs were desperate for. Chargon had almost lived in the saloon for three days now and air not thick with cigar or pipe smoke was a welcome shock to his system. Rubbing his face, he found himself looking at the shining coin in his hand once more. You could buy a lot of things with a gold coin and that was exactly what he wanted to do. He wanted a lot of very important things. Things that were vital for a professional gunman.

Chargon stepped down off the boardwalk into the dry baked street and headed for the general store and then went for a shave. He still had a few coins left for a steak dinner, just as the white-haired Gene Adams had suggested. As he left the dining-hall in the hotel he walked out into the street with his bedroll under his arm and headed toward the cattle pens near the railroad tracks. He moved even better now as his confidence seemed to be raging through his body.

The offices that were lined one by one along the large board building were still open for business and Chargon had some very special business with one of the many men who traded there. The gold lettering on the glass panel door read FRED C. SMITH and as Chargon entered he studied the small well-dressed man behind the large desk. Smith was not like the rest of the cattle agents in McCoy, and had learned his trade on the hard streets of the lower east side of New York docks. He had learned to steal to get what he wanted. No deal was too outrageous for him. The end result was all that mattered to him. It was he who had lured the tall Chargon into doing a few special jobs for him. Chargon had earned his money with his gun. It was after the last shooting that the gunman had executed for Fred C. Smith that he had become a drunk. These two very different men were in effect very much alike. They were both ruthless in their own ways: Chargon with his gun and Smith with his ambition.

Fred C. Smith's eyes watched as Chargon placed the bedroll onto his desk and sat down opposite him.

'You going somewhere, Chargon?' the small man enquired as he struck a match and lit his cigar.

'I got a proposition for you, Mr Smith.' He grinned from a face that was still shining from his recent encounter with a barber's straight razor.

'You have a proposition for me?' The small deceptive man seemed to be interested in the gunman's words.

'Yep. All you gotta do is supply me with enough money for a fresh horse and a lot of cartridges for my gun.' Chargon knew that he was sounding even more confident now.

'If I give you money you will probably go on another drunk like the last time.' Smith shook his head. 'Remember the last time? I do.'

'That was then.' Chargon leaned forward and stared hard into the man's face with an intensity that had long eluded him.

'Why would I want to give you money for a horse and bullets, Chargon?' Smith asked. 'You might just ride off and I would lose even more money.'

'Come with me then.' Chargon raised an eyebrow as if he was actually daring the businessman.

'Where are you going?' Smith was at last starting to become interested.

'I'm going after Adams.' Chargon smiled.

'Gene Adams? The same Gene Adams that brought in a herd of longhorns today?' Fred C. Smith rose up in his chair. 'Have you lost your mind, Chargon?'

'How much did he make today from you dealers?' Chargon asked, as if it made any real difference to either of them. The figure was unimportant.

Smith got to his feet and sucked on the long cigar as he moved to the window and stared at the pens full of prime beef on the hoof. 'He made a hell of a lot of money. What are you thinking of, Chargon?'

'I reckon I can take it off him.' Chargon was enthusiastic enough to warrant listening to.

'I hear he's fast and he's got a lot of men.' Smith was seriously considering the proposition as he sucked and blew the smoke of his expensive cigar.

'He paid them all off except for two.' The gunman was sweating with total confidence. Its aroma was filling the room with an air of evil that both men liked.

'So he has only two cowboys with him?' Smith sucked on the long rolled weed.

'Yep. Just two,' Chargon confirmed.

'Are they any good?'

'One is an old-timer and the other is a young kid.' Chargon stood and moved to the small man's side and joined him in viewing the cattle in the pens.

'A kid and an old man.' Smith put his hand inside his long coat and withdrew his thick wallet. Chargon watched as the man pulled out three fifty-dollar bills and held them out to him.

'So you like my idea, Mr Smith?' The gunman accepted the cash and smiled at the bills in his hand.

'It has its merits, Mr Chargon.' The small man nodded as he pushed his wallet back into his coat pocket.

'So we have a deal, Smith?' Chargon stuffed the three bills into his shirt pocket.

Smith pulled the cigar from his mouth and blew the smoke at the floor. 'Get two horses.'

'So you wanna join me on my little adventure?'

'There are so few adventures, Mr Chargon,' Smith raised his eyes to look at the gunman, 'it would be sad to miss out on this one.'

Chargon smiled again. 'This is going to be a very profitable partnership.'

'Fifty-fifty?'

'Agreed.'

Fred C. Smith watched as the tall man left the office and headed off towards the livery stables. He had never truly liked Gene Adams and his golden Colts. Smith had always liked the idea of having those weapons strapped around his middle where they would be far better suited. To take back all the company's gold that had been paid to the Bar 10 was also something that appealed to him. Even he was not stupid enough to imagine that this was going to be an easy undertaking but the sheer magnitude of the potential profit made it strangely fascinating.

Chargon was no normal gunhand. He had a past that was truly impressive to an Easterner like himself. Smith opened the top drawer of his desk and pulled out a gunbelt that he had purchased two years earlier when he had arrived from New York. He strapped it around his waist and studied the weapon for a while. This was going to be an experience that was almost too exciting for words and he knew a lot of words.

He donned his Stetson and locked the office door behind him before following in the direction that Chargon had taken only minutes earlier.

It may well have been only greed that spurred the man on but there was also the memories of all those dime novels by Ned Buntline that he had read avidly before heading West. This might be his one and only chance at making his mark.

Fred C. Smith seemed to get taller with every step he took as he closed in on the stables and the waiting Chargon.

5

Sutters Corner was an extremely quiet place. Few knew of this hotel and even fewer used it any longer. Sutters Corner had once been a small town but now only the small wooden-board hotel was occupied. The rest of the place was a string of empty buildings which the woodland was slowly reclaiming. There had once been gold claims dotted around the hillside but gradually they had dried up. One by one the miners left for richer pickings further west and civilization had followed the men with the goldpans and shovels. Only old man Davis remained in his once profitable hotel, too stubborn or too old to leave. His was a clean boarding-house that served its patrons well.

Gene Adams reined his mare to a halt and dismounted outside the building with flickering lamplight in its windows and smoke billowing from its chimney. The sun was almost gone but it got dark here earlier than down on the prairie due to the tall trees that covered the mountainside.

Tomahawk slid off his black horse with the agility of someone much younger and tied his reins to the hitching pole as the young Johnny Puma guided his pinto between the two other mounts. Johnny sat for a while studying the long empty street in front of the hotel and rubbed his neck. He had never seen any of those buildings occupied. To him, it had always been a ghost town.

'This place gives me the creeps,' he said as he dismounted from his pony.

'It was real fun in the olden days, boy,' Tomahawk said as he stepped up on to the raised boardwak.

'It was sure lively,' Adams chuckled.

'You old guys are always talking about the old days,' Johnny muttered to himself as he tied his reins firmly to the rail.

'Things back then were more fun.' The old man smiled.

'No they weren't, Tomahawk,' Gene Adams rebutted as he untied his saddle-bags from behind his saddle cantle along with his bedroll.

Johnny Puma untied the bulging saddle-bag from his pinto's back and pulled it down. Its sheer weight made it hit the ground before the young man could get a firm grip on it.

'Gold is sure heavy old stuff,' Tomahawk commented with a wry smile. 'Or is you getting weak, Johnny?'

'Don't pick on the boy, Tomahawk,' Adams teased. 'Gold is very heavy and our Johnny ain't fully grown yet.'

Johnny muttered under his breath as he followed the two older men up the wooden steps into the small hotel, struggling under the weight of the leather saddle-bags.

The interior of the building was very pleasing to the eye and reflected its glorious past. The decoration was typical of all hotels. Good thick wallpaper and even thicker paintwork. The red drapes that hung in various positions added a luxurious tone to the now ageing building.

They stood alone at the desk for several minutes waiting for signs of life. Johnny rested his heavy bags on the carpet at his feet and gave the place a better look as Tomahawk hit the bell on the desk.

The lounge seemed to stretch for over thirty feet to their left and only stopped at the huge window made up of over four dozen small panes of glass. To their right a broad wooden staircase covered in a worn red carpet rose elegantly to the second floor.

'Hit the bell again, Tomahawk,' Gene Adams sighed as he placed the saddle-bag at his feet. It had been a very long day that had started at dawn. Apart from a rushed breakfast provided by the chuck-wagon cook, none of the three men had eaten all day and it was starting to show.

The old-timer's hand was just about

to strike down upon the polished brass bell when the red velvet curtain behind the desk ruffled. The three men from the Bar 10 were expecting old man Davis to appear as he always did.

'Get your scrawny butt out here, Davis,' Tomahawk yelled at the moving red drape.

All three men's mouths fell open at the sight that confronted their trail-weary eyes. This was not old man Davis. This wasn't even a man. This was a beautiful girl of about twenty with long soft blonde hair and very green eyes, dressed in a white shirt tucked into blue jeans.

'Gosh,' Tomahawk gasped in surprise.

'Hello,' Johnny smiled as he removed his Stetson and stepped up to the desk with a gleam in his eyes.

'Hello,' the girl said reluctantly to the three strangers before her. She stepped to the desk and placed her small pale hands upon the wooden stained counter top and studied the trio very carefully.

'I'm sorry about my friend's rude words, ma'am,' Gene Adams apologized as he too removed his hat revealing his white neat hair. 'We thought you were old man Davis. He's an old friend of ours.'

She looked very nervously at them as she turned the large book around for them to sign.

'Who are you?' Johnny sighed.

'I'm Nancy Davis. His niece,' she replied as she watched Gene Adams remove his right glove, pick up the pen off the counter and dip it into the inkwell. 'He asked me to come out here and stay for a while.'

'Where is the old coyote?' Tomahawk asked.

Adams shook his head as he wrote on the book. 'I'll sign for my friends because my young friend Johnny is drooling too much to hold a pen and Tomahawk here can't write anyway.'

For the first time the young female

started to relax and smile at the new guests. Then they all heard a distinctive whistling coming from up the stairs. All four sets of eyes watched as the elderly hotelier came wandering down the carpeted stairs towards them.

'Gene, Tomahawk and Johnny,' Davis yelled at the top of his voice as he rushed toward the trio. 'Long time no see.'

'Eleven months, to be exact, Davis,' Adams said as he patted the man on his back.

'Why so long?' Davis asked.

'Well we ain't been in these parts since last year,' Adams explained. 'Last year we brought a pretty big herd to McCoy and we had to wait until we had enough steers to come back.'

'Uncle?' Nancy raised her small hand as she tried to get his attention.

The old man turned to his niece. 'What, Nancy dear?'

'Shall I prepare some food for these gentlemen?'

'Gentlemen?' Tomahawk started to

giggle. 'She called me a gentleman, Johnny. Did you hear her?'

Johnny was glowing as he watched Nancy starting to blush. 'I heard her, Tomahawk. She sounds real fine.'

Gene Adams looked at old man Davis and raised his black eyebrows which contrasted with his white hair. 'Johnny's in love again. I'm awful sorry.'

★   ★   ★

The meal had arrived less than an hour later and was better than anything any of the three men from the Bar 10 Ranch had ever tasted. Nancy Davis could cook as good as she looked, and she looked extremely good. As the three older men sat around the roaring fireplace and tossed even more logs into the centre of the flames, Johnny Puma excused himself and made his way outside into the moonlight. Standing upon the porch staring at the ghost town before him he tried to imagine this place when it had been a town with blood in its veins. However hard he tried, he could see nothing but the dereliction before him.

He wondered about the strange figure of Chargon who had made trouble back in McCoy earlier. He remembered Chargon, as he knew Chargon recalled him. Those were days when he lived by his wits and the speed of his guns. Those were days he had long forgotten and wished had never happened. Yet they had happened and Chargon had been there to witness them. Those were times before he had drifted on to the Bar 10 Ranch and met up with the calming influence and faith of the tall, shrewd Gene Adams. Without Gene Adams there would have been no Johnny Puma and probably no more drifting. Even though he had been very young he had courted the wrong side of the law and somehow meeting Adams had changed him. Johnny Puma knew that it would only be a matter of time before he encountered someone like Chargon from his past. Although he had known it, when it actually happened, it left a sour taste in his mouth.

'Hard to believe that this place was once a thriving little community, isn't it?' The soft voice came from the shadows and for a second made the young cowboy jump before his eyes focused upon her sitting on the two-seater swing that hung from the overhanging porch canopy.

'Nancy,' Johnny sighed to himself, as his fingers twitched above his guns. He was jumpy and felt stupid to have been on the verge of drawing his forty-fives on such a sweet young female. 'I didn't see you there.'

'Did I startle you, Johnny?' she asked quietly.

Embarrassed by his stupidity he moved toward her and held on to one of the swing's chains. 'Yep. You scared me, Miss Davis.'

'My name is Nancy, Johnny.' She said with insistence in her voice, 'Please call me Nancy.'

'Sure, eh . . . Nancy,' he stammered.

She looked out at the view before them and sighed heavily as if regretting arriving at Sutters Corner too late. 'I find this a sad place. So very, very sad, Johnny. Where did all the people go?'

'Spooky is the word I'd use.' He grinned down upon her as if inhaling every ounce of her being into his nostrils. He had been in love many times and it only took a girl as pretty as her to make him start to feel his juices brewing.

She giggled. 'Yes, it is spooky.'

'I never seen Sutters Corner in its prime, like Gene and Tomahawk,' he admitted, looking down on her beautiful head perched daintily on top of her beautiful body.

She stared up at the young man with a look of a woman who had not seen an eligible male for far too long. 'So you are a real cowboy, Johnny?'

'Yep.' He found it hard to deny the obvious and he was starting to find it almost impossible denying her anything at all. She just looked and smelled too good.

'Very romantic.' She patted the bench beside her as if inviting him to sit down. He did so quickly.

'Being a cowboy ain't very romantic, Nancy,' he admitted. 'I guess I can see how folks from back East could imagine it, though.'

'How did you know I was from back East?' She looked surprised.

'You talk faster than women around these parts, Nancy.' He gave a grin that was returned with interest.

'Is that a good thing?'

'It's mighty fine.' Johnny touched the ends of her long blonde hair with his fingers. 'Mighty fine.'

'The prairie and the stars,' she sighed, waving her arms around as if pointing. 'What on earth could be more romantic than that?'

'Sitting on a porch in the moonlight with a very pretty gal is what I call romantic,' he said, thinking about his life. 'I've been eating trail-dust riding drag behind five thousand head of longhorns for the past few weeks. That ain't romantic at all, Nancy.'

'You like it though.' She heaved her chest.

'I've had worse jobs.' Johnny Puma knew they were the truest words he had spoken all night.

'You look healthy and strong,' she commented, touching his forearms delicately with her long slim fingers.

'I guess so.' He could not take his eyes off her soft hair and the subtle perfume that scented her body. 'Wrestling longhorns tends to build anyone up if you do it long enough.'

Nancy turned her head until the light of the moon twinkled in her eyes at him. 'You are very, very handsome, Johnny.'

'You ain't met many men lately, have you?' He smiled with a coyness that had melted many a female heart.

'Oh I've met quite a few, Johnny. I'm serious though, you are very, very handsome.' Nancy Davis had a sound in her voice that the young trail-weary cowboy had not heard for quite a while. It was the sound of a real woman and not the usual bargirls whom he bumped into regularly.

'You sure look mighty tempting, Nancy.'

'You talk a lot for a cowboy, Johnny.' Her eyes started to close as she leaned toward his strong body. 'Why don't you do something else with that mouth of yours?'

He decided that it was not worth arguing with such a beautiful female. He pulled her close and their lips met. Johnny Puma had kissed a lot of girls before but this was the first time he felt as if he was being kissed back. She tasted good. Very, very good indeed.

6

The noise that came from down the long deserted street which faced the old hotel at Sutters Corner caused the young cowboy to release his grip on Nancy Davis and walk to the edge of the porch steps. His face went taut as he strained his eyes to see something in the blue shadows. Moonlight could be romantic but could also be infuriating when you tried to focus tired eyes.

'What was that, Johnny?' the young woman asked as she clung to his arm. 'I'm scared.'

Johnny Puma blew out long and hard as he tried to think of an answer for her.

'What the heck was that, Johnny?' Nancy Davis repeated her question. This time there was a chilling tone to her voice. She was scared and if the truth were known, so was the cowboy.

'I ain't sure, Nancy,' he replied

quietly. 'Get Gene and Tomahawk.'

Nancy Davis rushed into the building as the wall clock struck ten and spoke to the three men who were seated before the fireplace. Within seconds all three were standing next to Johnny Puma, wondering what was wrong.

'What's the matter, Johnny?' Gene Adams asked as he stared in the same direction as his young friend. 'What spooked you and Nancy?'

'This town is supposed to be deserted?' Johnny glanced at Adams briefly.

'Yep,' Gene Adams confirmed.

'It ain't. We got company.' Johnny held on to the handles of his guns as he spoke. 'Didn't you hear the noise?'

'What noise, Johnny?'

'It came from down there.' The young cowboy nodded to indicate the direction.

Adams rested a calming hand upon his young friend's shoulder and tried to make light of the youngster's concern.

'It must have been the wind or something.'

Tomahawk moved closer to the porch rail. 'There ain't no wind, Gene. Not even a breeze.'

'He's right,' old man Davis agreed, holding his niece's hand firmly.

'What did you hear, Johnny?' Gene Adams quietly asked his saddle chum.

'A loud noise, Gene.' The young man rested the palms of his hands upon the handles of his pistol.

'It was very loud, Mister Adams,' Nancy said in a breathless voice.

'It might have been a coyote or something knocking over . . . '

Another noise rang out through the street. Its echo vibrated around the five souls on the hotel porch. Gene Adams drew one of his gold plated forty-fives and looked at his companion.

'Davis? Take Nancy inside,' he said. 'Me and the boys are gonna check out what in tarnation that is.' He spoke in a masterful tone that only came from men who have lived long and hard by never running away from their fears.

Adams walked down into the street, past their horses, with Tomahawk at his heels and the youthful Johnny Puma moving wide to their left. They moved slowly down the deserted street using the shadows of the ghost town's buildings as cover from their unseen enemies.

Another loud noise made all three men freeze in their tracks momentarily as they tried to figure out where exactly the sound had come from. It was Adams who first seemed to be confident of having worked out the general direction of the sound. He pointed with his gun down the long boardwalk at the very last building, which had once been the sheriff's office.

Tomahawk nodded in agreement with his boss and headed after the silver-haired man towards the building. The young Johnny Puma was less certain but he too moved to where Gene Adams had pointed with the golden gun.

All three men approached the small sheriff's office with guns drawn. The boardwalk before the office was rotten and had only half its original boards remaining, so the three had to be extra careful as they stepped up from the street to gain entry into the building.

As they got to the open doorway, Adams raised his gloved left hand up to his two friends and watched as they stopped. He crouched again and peered around the frame of the door into the darkness. He could not see anything odd at all. Tomahawk's eyes searched his boss for indications as to what their next move was but nothing came back from the silver-haired man.

For a moment Gene Adams's brain raced, wondering what to do next as he hovered near the base of the door-frame upon the creakingly unsteady cross-joists. The moonlight gleamed over their shoulders making them far from invisible and the tension began to rise as they waited for something to give them a clue as to what to do next.

Then it happened.

A thunderous volley of Winchester fire sprayed through the open doorway, causing Adams and his two friends to take desperate cover. Adams went low between the joists whilst Tomahawk and Johnny threw themselves down to the side of the jailhouse, using its dried up water-trough as their shield.

The bullets that blasted out from the darkness made red hot traces in the cold night air.

Then they heard another sort of noise coming from within the small building: the noise of someone smashing their way out through the rear door of the sheriff's office. Gene Adams crawled on all fours under the porch and looked down the side of the building. The long black shadows hid almost everything from his tired eyes. Almost everything but not quite all. The mature cattleman caught a brief glimpse of a figure dashing from behind one building to the next. He got to his feet and raised his gun to fire but it was too late. Whoever it was had gone.

'Come on, boys,' Adams yelled to his companions. Johnny and Tomahawk quickly got to their feet and rushed to Gene Adams's side. All three men ran up the dark alley to the rear of the old buildings and then followed Adams's lead. He alone had caught a glimpse of the figure who had been running through the darkness and he alone had seen which way the figure had gone.

'This way, boys,' he said quietly, pointing with the gold-plated barrel of the gun in his hand. Cautiously, all three made their way down the twisting overgrown alley in search of the varmint who had tried to blow their heads off.

Just as they had run about twenty feet after the mysterious figure, another volley of rifle bullets came hurtling at them from the hidden gunman. Adams dropped to the floor on to his belly and started to return the fire. Tomahawk slipped sideways behind an old water-barrel and the youthful Johnny Puma moved up against the wall of the old sheriff's office. Both men started to return fire down the almost black alleyway over their boss's head. Shot after shot left their pistols but there was no response. Suddenly Gene Adams raised his gloved hand.

'Stop firing, boys,' he ordered. 'Whoever it was has lit out.'

'You sure about that, Gene?' Tomahawk peeked around the side of the barrel at his friend who had already risen to his feet. 'I ain't in the mood to get ventilated.'

'I'm sure.' Adams strolled back to the old-timer, held out a hand and helped the bearded man up. He holstered his weapons and gave Johnny Puma a glance as he moved from out of the shadows toward them.

'Did you see who it was?' Johnny asked, still holding both his guns tightly.

'Nope,' Adams replied. 'All I saw was hot lead flying at us at one heck of a speed.'

'Let's check this old office out to see

what that varmint was doing,' Tomahawk suggested as he moved cautiously towards the rear door of the jailhouse.

Peering into the dark interior of the building through the busted rear door, Gene Adams shook his head. 'It's too damn dark to see anything tonight, boys. We'll check it out in the morning before we head on to the Bar 10.'

'What was all the noise, Gene?' Tomahawk asked, scratching his head.

'I figure that critter was looking for something,' Adams replied.

The three men made their way tentatively back up the quiet street using the dark shadows as cover, just in case whoever had opened up on them with the repeating carbine was still around.

Adams's eyes flashed frenziedly into every small corner of the deserted street as they walked back towards the hotel and its welcoming glowing lights. His guns were now holstered but his hands were never more than an inch away from their handles and triggers. Gene

Adams led his two men back to the relative safety of the small hotel with more questions in his brain than he had answers. In fact, he had no answers at all as to what had just occurred down the street and that bothered him.

He was last to walk up the steps of the hotel behind Johnny and Tomahawk. His ears strained to hear something — anything — that he might take aim at, but there was nothing. Stopping on the top step of the porch he gazed around the scene wondering who and why they had come under fire.

As he finally entered the hotel and felt the heat from the large log fire warming his bones, he began to settle down.

'What the heck was all that shooting, Gene?' old man Davis enquired, proffering a stiff drink.

'Whatever it was, it was no ghost,' Adams said thoughtfully, looking at the roaring blaze in the large stone fireplace.

'Take this drink. It'll warm you up.'

Davis was shocked when Adams shook his head, moved to the warmth of the fire and rested his gloved hand on the split log mantel, set into the stone fireplace.

'The fire will warm me up plenty,' Gene Adams sighed, staring into the flames as they danced around the wood.

Tomahawk took the glass from the hotelier and swilled it down his throat quickly. 'Gene don't drink liquor.'

Johnny Puma stood by the doorway staring out thoughtfully into the moon-lit scenery. 'I'll tend to the horses, Gene.'

Tomahawk followed the youngster. 'I'll help you, boy.'

As the door closed, Nancy Davis appeared with a tray of cups and a pot of coffee. She hesitated for an instant before moving to her uncle and the silent figure of Gene Adams, who was still staring hard into the flames as if trying to find answers to all his questions. She rested the tray down on the small table next to the long couch and then sat down. Her eyes watched the tall man.

'What was out there, Mr Adams?' she asked in a low soft voice.

Adams turned slowly and glanced down at her. 'I wish I knew, Nancy. I just wish I knew.'

'What was all the shooting for?' She seemed to be terrified at the question that had just left her lips.

'Some critter opened up on us with a carbine.' Adams shook his head as he leaned down and poured himself a hot coffee. 'I guess we scared somebody enough to make them wanna fill us full of lead.'

Davis sat down next to his niece before staring hard into the rancher's face. 'You shoot back?'

'We did. We were as accurate as the critter that was shooting at us.' Adams gave a small laugh. 'It was pretty dark though.'

Davis looked hard at his old friend.

'What would anyone want to shoot at you for, Gene?'

'Whoever it was would have spit lead at anyone.' Adams gave a long hard sigh. 'Somebody was sure eager to find something down there. Something worth shooting strangers for.'

'Who could it have been?' Nancy looked from her uncle to Adams and back once again. Both men were as bemused as she.

Neither had any answer for the beautiful young woman.

7

Dawn had arrived and the three riders from the Bar 10 were already wide awake. They had eaten their breakfast and vacated their room with their two bulging saddle-bags in tow. Tomahawk had saddled the three horses in the hotel stables before bringing them round to the front of the building. He tied them to the hitching rail outside the front of the hotel, whilst he watched Gene Adams and Johnny Puma descending the wooden steps from the porch with the hefty bags. After heaving the two bags up onto the back of the saddles behind their bedrolls and securing them, the two men joined Tomahawk. He was staring out at the ghost town with an expression that seemed out of place upon his craggy whiskered face. For the first time in a long time he looked worried.

Gene Adams rested a hand upon the old man's shoulder. 'You ready to have a look around, Tomahawk?'

Tomahawk shrugged. 'Guess so.'

The old man did not seem to Adams to be as confident as he usually was. Adams was concerned. He had known the grizzly old mountain man for too long to miss the signs of his being very, very worried.

'You could stay here if you want,' Adams said quietly. 'Me and Johnny can check out things down there.'

'I'm coming with you critters.' Tomahawk spat into the sand and gave his usual grin. 'What would you boys do without me along? You need a man who is good with his gun. A man who is faster than lightning on the draw.'

Adams put his gloved hand over the bearded mouth to silence the old-timer. 'Shut up.'

Johnny Puma checked his guns were fully loaded as the three men started the long walk down the eerily empty street. He was silent as if straining to hear the slightest noise that would warn him of danger. All that any of the three cowboys could hear was the birds singing upon every branch in every tree.

'Damn birds,' Johnny muttered as they moved down the street at a steady, controlled pace.

'Easy, Johnny,' Adams said to his young friend. 'Use your eyes. The sound of birds can't affect your eyesight.'

Johnny followed the two older men as they moved across to the left side of the street and on toward the sheriff's office. He used his eyes. Nothing escaped him.

Tomahawk held on to his forty-five with one hand whilst he rested the palm of his other on top of his hatchet. He had not been so nervous in many a long time. Years of tending steers had made him soft, at least soft by his own high standards.

Adams pulled his right hand gun from its holster as they drew ever closer to the ramshackle old jailhouse. His eyes were almost closed as he concentrated on the buildings around them as they paced. Each step seemed to ring a bell within each man's soul, warning of impending doom.

However curious Gene and his men were, they were cowboys by trade and not investigators. All they had on their side was the fact that before any of them had set eyes upon a steer, they had lived often dangerous lives. No amount of trail drives could wash that out of their veins.

Suddenly there was a rustling sound to their right and Tomahawk raised his pistol and fired instinctively at the sound.

The tumbleweed rolled past their feet taking no notice of the bullet that had just passed through it. Pausing for a moment, all three men looked at each other.

'Well?' Tomahawk sniffed at his friends. 'It might have been that dang varmint that shot at us last night.'

Gene Adams patted his old friend on

the back. 'Very true.'

'At least I hit it,' Tomahawk grumbled.

'You killed that damn tumbleweed stone dead, Tomahawk.' Johnny found himself smiling for the first time since he had awoken. 'You can sure kill tumbleweed. That's a fact.'

'Accurate.' Adams joined in the gentle teasing of their old pal. 'Our Tomahawk is pretty accurate with his old Colt.'

'I was dang quicker with my gun than either of you two old cowpunchers,' Tomahawk snarled as they slowly continued their advance down the godforsaken street.

'Faster than Jesse James, I reckon,' Johnny laughed.

The morning sun was warm and welcome as they finally reached their objective. The old sheriff's office stood in a sorrowfully sad state before them. Adams was the first to enter, with his friends close behind. They stopped and studied the interior carefully for quite some time.

To the surprise of all three there was nothing in the old jailhouse to warrant anyone making such a racket as the very mysterious rifleman had done the previous evening.

'Ain't nothing here, Gene.' Tomahawk scratched his head in confusion.

Adams said nothing for a moment as his eyes surveyed everything within the confines of the small building.

'Maybe the varmint found what he was looking for and lit out with it,' Johnny Puma surmised.

'That could be it.' Tomahawk nodded at the youngster before turning to his boss. 'Do you reckon Johnny is right, Gene?'

Adams rested his hip on the crumbling old desk and rubbed his chin with his gloved hand. 'Maybe.'

'What's wrong, Gene?' Johnny asked as he noted the expression upon his friend's face. 'You look troubled.'

'I am, Johnny.' Adams chewed his bottom lip.

'What for?' Tomahawk moved closer to his two pals.

'What could have been in here that was so darn important that some critter was willing to kill us for?' Adams stared through his dark eyebrows at the other two.

Both men were silent. Neither could come up with a reasonable explanation and they waited silently until Gene Adams stood and went back out into the deserted street. They followed the tall man out into the bright sunshine that had now lifted above the tall trees surrounding Sutters Corner. The walk down the alleyway revealed the many tracks in the sand of the previous night's action. Adams led his companions to the point where they had lost the rifleman. He could see where the man had knelt and where he had run to. They soon found the hoof-marks where the man had lit out. At the end of their investigation they were none the wiser.

The slow walk back to the hotel was

filled with thoughts that led absolutely nowhere.

After paying their bill, Adams walked out of Davis's hotel and mounted his chestnut mare. Tomahawk was already waiting in his saddle upon his black gelding. Both men stared at each other as they waited for the young man with more on his mind than mysterious gunmen.

'Why we waiting?' Tomahawk asked his friend. 'As if I didn't know.'

'Johnny is bidding Nancy farewell, Tomahawk.' Gene smiled as he sat leaning back against his saddle cantle checking the saddle-bag was tied securely.

Johnny Puma came out of the hotel door with the beautiful blonde Nancy upon his arm. Neither of the mounted cowboys could bring themselves to watch exactly how many times the youngsters' lips met before Johnny finally managed to free himself from her willing grasp. As the young man mounted his pinto, she clung to his jeaned leg as if trying to persuade him to stay for a little dessert.

'We'll be back, Miss Nancy,' Adams grinned in a fatherly way down at the young lady. His words did not seem totally to convince her.

'When will you get back here, Johnny?' Her voice begged for an answer.

'Pretty soon.' Johnny touched her lips with his fingers and pulled his mount away from the rail. 'I'll get back here as soon as I can. That's a promise.'

As Tomahawk followed the young rider, Gene Adams paused on his mare beside the lovely female and looked down at her.

'I'll send him over here in a couple of weeks on an errand for the Bar 10, Nancy.' He grinned and she returned it with a grateful smile.

Adams spurred his horse gently and cantered after the other two. They headed along the winding trail that led them toward the prairie. Adams held his reins tightly as they rode at a reasonable speed through the trees. This was no easy route but it was by far the safest way until they reached the wide, almost flat desert that they had to use when they were driving herds.

No other riders had used this trail for a very long time as was evident by the state of the track. It was thick with weeds and overgrown up to their horses' shoulders.

Somehow, Gene Adams was able to persuade his mare to forge ahead even through the roughest terrain without ever resorting to violence. This man was a leader; others followed. Tomahawk followed faithfully whilst Johnny Puma trailed last with thoughts of what he had left behind at Sutters Corner hotel.

Within an hour they had left the woodland that skirted the mountain near Sutters Corner and had reached the flat wide prairie which was over three miles across at its widest point. Now they rode side by side at a speed that would make up for their losing so much time earlier.

The trail began to narrow as they rode ever closer to Devil's Canyon. Beyond the canyon they could take a short cut that would lead them to the Bar 10 much more quickly than the route they had to take when they were driving a large herd. They would be able to head over Devil's Bluff, a vast mountain range that was ideal for riders in a hurry, as they were. It was still a couple of days' ride before they could reach the Bar 10 but they would stop at a small cantina they knew of high in the dry mountain range that night. They still had a very long hard ride before they could reach the cantina. They hoped that they would get there before dark.

8

Fred C. Smith had never ridden so far or so long in all his life as he had done during the last twenty-four hours. Following the determined Chargon had seemed like a very good idea back in McCoy before the saddle sores had started to bleed inside his tailored pants. For some reason they had ridden all through the night and even the newly restored Chargon could not see tracks in the darkness. The two men had finally come to a halt just short of the large waterfall that cascaded from the mountains and forests of Sutters Corner. They were on the dry prairie and had ridden along the wide flat cattle-trail that Adams had used to bring his steers to market. The waterfall was the only sign of life in this desolate place as the saddle-weary Smith fell painfully from his horse. His knees could hardly straighten as he creaked around towards the welcoming sight of the pool before him. His horse trotted to the cool stream that led away from the pool and started to drink while its master groaned with every step towards the drink he so badly wanted.

Thirst and pain did not seem to enter into Chargon's thoughts as he sat silently upon his horse, watching his travelling companion and newly found partner stagger towards the water.

'You OK, Smith?' he asked as he dismounted.

Fred C. Smith fell on to his knees, submerged his face into the cold water and drank.

Chargon removed his canteen off the saddle horn, kneeled down beside Smith and started to fill it. His eyes were as keen now as they had been when they had started out on their quest. He looked up to the top of the waterfall and the trees that covered everything before him over the deep pond. Then he turned and gazed at the arid wasteland of the prairie behind him. Nothing seemed to grow there for mile after dusty mile and the heat made it shimmer.

Smith pulled himself up from the water and rolled over on to his back, gasping. The sun burned down on his face as he took deep breath after deep breath.

'You thinking what I'm thinking?' Chargon muttered as he screwed the top back on to his canteen.

'What you thinking?' Smith gasped.

'We ain't behind Adams.' Chargon took a handful of water and sipped it.

'We must be,' Smith whined. 'We've been riding all damn night.'

'We have but what if they haven't?' Chargon stood and hung the dripping canteen back over the horn before kneeling down again next to the cool waterhole.

'You mean we rode past them during the night?' Smith rose to a sitting position. His face was wet but still showed his fury.

Chargon shook his head.

'What then?' Smith yelled as he felt the blood in his pants stinging.

'Up there in the woods is an old ghost town called Sutters Corner and there used to be a hotel,' Chargon explained. 'What if that old rascal Adams went there rather than along here?'

'So he's gone by a different route?' Smith raised his arms into the air and clenched his fists. 'That's perfect, Chargon. Just damn perfect.'

'Quit hollering, Smith.' Chargon took water in both his hands, raised them to his mouth again and drank.

'Quit hollering? Quit hollering?' Smith was gritting his teeth as he tried to move but failed. 'I got no skin left on my butt and you say quit hollering.'

'We ain't lost them.' Chargon winked.

'We ain't?'

'They got to come back down on to this plain to continue on.' Chargon was grinning. 'There ain't no other way but to head down here.'

'So?' Smith was totally confused.

'So we are in front of them by my figuring.'

'We are?' Fred C. Smith found himself smiling through his pain.

'We must be.' Chargon grabbed another handful of water and flicked it into Smith's face.

'Don't you ever do that again, Chargon,' Smith said as the water ran down his cheeks.

Chargon laughed and got to his feet. 'This might be just about the best situation we could be in, Mister Fred C. Smith.'

Smith staggered to his feet. 'How so?'

'Ever heard of the word bushwhack before?'

'I like it.' Smith grinned greedily.

'They gotta come here to water their horses and fill their canteens before they head into the Devil's Canyon.' Chargon stretched his arms as if in triumph.

Suddenly thoughts filled the mind of

Smith. Thoughts of his name being blazed across dime novels back east for all to read about how he was famous like all those he had once read about.

'Very good, Chargon,' he oozed.

★   ★   ★

It so happened that neither Smith nor the gunman Chargon had very long to wait before their tired eyes spied the sight that cheered them both up. The trail dust drifted in the still air away from the three riders who were coming down the centre of the arid plain.

It was Chargon who first noticed the distant riders and pointed with his long crooked trigger finger. Fred C. Smith stood wide-legged next to the taller, leaner, man, squinting as hard as he could. His eyes were not as adept as his new-found partner's.

'See them?'

'I see dust rising but . . . ' Smith was unsure of what he was looking at but trusted his less civilized companion to

85

fill in the gaps caused by his own bookkeeper's eyes.

'That's Adams and his cronies, Smith.' Chargon spat on the ground in front of them confidently.

Smith shrugged. 'You can see that far?'

'Sure,' Chargon snorted.

'You can actually see that those distant dots are Adams and his men?' Smith turned away from the glaring desert and made his way to the sweet water of the pond.

'It has to be Adams, don't it?' Chargon rubbed his burning eyes as he continued to stare through the heat haze. He was not really sure of what he was looking at except that it was three men mounted on horses. Logic told him that this had to be Gene Adams and his two men heading home to Texas.

'Guess so.' Smith drew his gun and checked it over before spinning its ammunition chamber.

The tall man moved to the water and

stared at Smith with cold hard eyes. 'Can you use that thing or will I have to do the shooting for both of us?'

Fred C. Smith was silent as he span the pistol on his index finger expertly before dropping it neatly into its holster.

'Well?' Smith asked quietly.

Chargon raised his eyebrows. 'You'll do.'

The approaching riders were heading for the waterfall as all travellers did. Chargon took both horses and led them down the trail for a few yards before enshrouding them within the thick bushes. He tied their reins to the saplings near the water's edge before returning to the still saddle-sore Smith.

'We better take advantage of the cover around here,' the tall man advised.

Smith gazed out at the desert plain before removing his coat and tossing it over his shoulder.

'We got time yet, Chargon.'

'They'll be here in about thirty

minutes, friend.'

'You reckon?'

'I reckon.'

Smith nodded to his companion's greater knowledge before looking around the area for a suitable place to hide. He was not very experienced when it came to bushwhacking.

'What's our plan?'

Chargon shook his weary head. 'I'll light out to the right and you go to the left.'

'And?'

'When they is in the middle, we opens up.' Chargon could taste the gold coins that were motivating his every move. 'Get it, my small buddy?'

'How close should we let them get before we opens up?' Smith was very concerned that if he started shooting too early everything might just go haywire and they would end up on the receiving end. Adams was no mug. Adams was pretty darn useful with his weapons and he had two very skilful men with him. It all seemed to be getting rather close to dangerous for the New Yorker. Plus, he was starting to wonder if his one six-shooter was a match for the unique pair of gold-plated Colts that hung from Adams's belt.

'Why you sweating, Smith?' Chargon stepped close to the smaller man and ran his fingers up the side of the man's sweating face. 'You ain't going yellow, are you?'

'No. I'm just starting to get very worried that this might be a foolhardy action on our part.' Fred C. Smith gave a gulp as he talked. 'Adams is pretty good with them irons of his, I hear.'

'You remember what you heard about me and my gun?' Chargon put his arm around Smith's shoulder and gave him a squeeze. 'I'm good with my gun too.'

'Yes, but we only have two weapons between us.'

'I only need one gun,' Chargon grunted in self-satisfaction as he held his partner tightly. 'Only bad shots need two pistols.'

'Is that so?'

'Yep.' Chargon pointed to a large boulder that lay amid thick weeds and sapling trees. 'You hide in there whilst I find a good spot that'll give me a clear aim at Adams and his cronies.'

Smith did as he was told and moved to the boulder. Then the sky began to darken over their heads as a storm brewed up and started to spit rain down upon them. As he got to the large boulder and turned, he was shocked that Chargon was nowhere to be seen. Through the pouring rain, he had no idea where his fellow bushwhacker was hiding.

Suddenly, Fred C. Smith felt very relieved. If Chargon was that good they just might have a chance at getting away with this outrage, he considered.

For the next thirty-three minutes the rain continued to crash down upon them as lightning occasionally flashed and thunder roared over the high waterfall. Steam rose off the hot baked ground as the rain teemed down. Both men were soaked to the skin several times over before they heard the sound of horses snorting restlessly as they came toward the oasis.

The animals caused even more steam to fill the clearing between Smith's hiding place and Chargon's. They could see the men wearing their waterproofs dismounting from the tired beasts.

Then it happened. Chargon started to fire and after a brief moment, Smith joined in blindly. The gunsmoke mixed with the creatures' steam and after both men had emptied their weapons nothing could be seen for several minutes. Smith managed somehow to reload his gun although by the time he slid the sixth bullet into its chamber he realized that everything was silent in the clearing.

The constant rainfall hit his face hard and stung his skin as he peered out from behind the boulder for the first time since the shooting had started.

His eyes widened as he focused on the sight before him. In the mud into which the dry sand had turned as soon as the rain had started to hit it, lay three bodies. One of the horses had fallen next to them as it had been caught in the crossfire. Smith rose from his kneeling position and felt both his knees creak as he straightened up. He stood for a while just looking down at the carnage before his still-smoking pistol as the relentless rain washed over him. The steam continued rising from the creatures even in death and the New Yorker could smell the warm blood that ebbed from each of the bodies around him.

Even the rain could not wash away the feeling that crept over Fred C. Smith as he caught sight of Chargon coming out of the bushes with a broad smile across his face.

'We did it, partner,' Chargon shouted over the sound of the steady downpour. 'We did it good.'

Smith nodded, finding himself unable

to speak. His eyes flashed around the wet scene and he saw the other two horses standing less than twenty feet away. They had not run away even during the horrendous bushwhacking, but stayed close to their dead masters.

Chargon reloaded his pistol as he got close to the shaking Smith, who stood like a statue before the horrific scene.

'You OK?'

'Fine,' Smith croaked as he felt his throat tighten.

'Nothing like a good killing to make you feel alive, I always say.' Chargon was laughing as he knelt down to the body of the nearest man covered in a huge waterproof. He holstered his gun and turned the body over.

It was then that Smith heard the laughter cease.

'Something wrong?' Smith edged closer to his kneeling partner as the rain started to ease up slightly.

Chargon was motionless for a long time before he rose to his feet mumbling as he made his way to the second body. He repeated his actions once more and was mumbling as he went to the third body.

'What's wrong, Chargon?' Smith shouted at the brooding man who was standing looking up at the rain with clenched fists.

Chargon turned slowly and stared at Smith. The small New Yorker had never before seen such an expression upon any living man's face. It was a look of anger and fury mixed with self-pity and confusion. As the rain beat at both their faces the taller man mumbled,

'We done killed three strangers, Smith. Three total strangers.'

Smith took the words in and rushed to the bodies himself, checking each of the three faces. The gunman was correct. They had gunned down three men that neither of them knew.

'Where the hell is Adams and his men?' Smith moved closer to his partner, who seemed in total shock.

'We done bushwhacked and killed

three strangers, Smith,' Chargon said as if in a trance. 'We killed the wrong men.'

Smith gritted on his teeth. 'Snap out of it, Chargon.'

Chargon looked down into Smith's face and shook his head as if unable to think clearly.

'What'll we do?' Smith shouted.

'We better clean up this mess.' Chargon grunted. 'Adams is coming this way. I can smell him.'

9

The storm clouds had passed by and the prairie was beginning to dry out as Gene Adams and his two companions found themselves within sight of the distant oasis. It was late afternoon before the three riders from the Bar 10 caught a glimpse of the far-off waterfall. They had been riding steadily towards it for several hours and were already beginning to smell the dampness of its vapour in their dust-clogged nostrils. They had been slowed up when they were forced to get their waterproofs out of their bedrolls as the storms started and then had to waste even more time putting them away again.

Gene Adams knew it would be more than an hour before they could fill their canteens with the cold clear water if they continued riding at their present speed and he was just about to suggest they increase their pace, when he reined hard, bringing his mare to an abrupt stop. Tomahawk pulled hard on his reins within seconds. Johnny Puma did not stop but circled his pony until he came up behind his friends.

All three men sat in their saddles silently staring ahead. Only Adams knew why they had stopped and he was standing in his stirrups shielding his eyes from the relentless beating of the sun. Even through the shimmering heat haze that lay between them and the distant mountain range and waterfall his eyes had spotted something out of place.

'What's the matter, Gene?' Johnny asked as he drew his pinto alongside the chestnut.

'Yeah, why did we stop?' Tomahawk asked, spitting the dust out of his dry mouth.

Adams sat down and pulled up his canteen and slowly unscrewed the stopper before taking a long hard drink of water. He was still watching the far-off waterfall and heavily wooded mountain but now seemed less surprised. 'Do both you boys require eye glasses?'

'What?'

'What you mean, Gene?'

Adams pointed at the tempting sight down the trail. Both men stared then shrugged before turning back to Adams who was returning his canteen to the horn of the saddle.

'I give up,' Johnny grinned.

'Me too.' Tomahawk picked up his canteen and shook it before opening its top and swigging.

'What springs to mind when you see a bunch of buzzards circling?' Adams pulled at the gloves ensuring they were tight across his skin. 'Come on boys, try to think.'

'Buzzards? I see what you mean.' Johnny squinted at the far away waterfall.

'Exactly.' Adams checked his guns in succession.

'What in tarnation you gabbing about

birds for?' Tomahawk said after he had swilled out his dust-caked mouth. 'What has birds got to do with anything?'

Johnny rubbed his chin. 'Trouble. That's what Gene means, Tomahawk.'

'Trouble? What sort of trouble?' Tomahawk hung his canteen by its long leather strap on the leather saddle horn.

'So, we have circling buzzards and what does that suggest to you, Tomahawk?' Gene Adams leaned across from his mount and rested his gloved hand on the old-timer's shoulder until Tomahawk made eye contact. 'Maybe something is pretty dead on the ground down there. Something dead near the waterfall, my old friend.'

'Yeah?' Tomahawk tried vainly to see what they were talking about but his eyes were just too old for the job. 'So that's why we stopped.'

'Exactly.' Gene Adams straightened up in his saddle.

'So what's the problem, Gene?' Johnny Puma gritted his teeth.

'Well, I just thought that if some critter got killed by maybe our rifle-toting friend from back at the ghost town, we might be riding into trouble,' Adams explained. 'So I figured I'd tell you both rather than let us ride on and get blown out of our saddles.'

All three men regretted their not having a Winchester between them but they seldom required their six-shooters, let alone carbines.

'So we gonna sit out here in this hot desert until we fry like eggs on a cooking range?' Tomahawk snorted.

'Nope.' Adams gathered up his reins and pulled his mare's head to their left. 'Follow me.'

The two cowboys did as they were told and trailed the chestnut mare as Gene Adams rode hard towards the thick woodland. It was a distance only just a little shorter than proceeding on towards the oasis.

Adams rode hard until they were below the steep tree-covered embankment that rose high above them. He reined and dismounted from the horse quickly. His two men followed suit.

'Now what?' Johnny enquired.

Gene Adams pointed up before turning to the two of them with a smile upon his face.

'We ain't going in there with these horses are we?' Tomahawk gulped, taking off his hat and beating the dust from it against his leg.

Gene Adams nodded. 'Give the old rooster a prize.'

10

To anyone else it might have seemed a crazy idea but not to the experienced Gene Adams. He was leading his mare along the narrow trail that led ever upward to the top of the mountain range. It mattered little to him how many trees or brambles there were in this virginal land, he wanted to get above the waterfall so that he could get a clear look at what was lurking below. It was obvious to his clear mind that somebody was waiting for them and their gold at the watering-hole and there just was no other way of playing safe.

The journey was a tortuous one that took several long hours but as each of the three men led their horses along the steep narrow trail they benefited from the coolness of the shadows cast by the thousands of tall thin pines.

By the time they reached a point where the ground levelled out they were totally exhausted but safe. The river that fed the waterfall was narrow but extremely fast moving. Gene Adams turned to his men and gave them one of his 'I told you we could do it' looks. After letting the beasts drink their fill the three men filled their canteens and sat getting their wind back.

It took a long time before any of them felt the strength returning to their weary legs. They were cowboys in high-heeled boots designed to slip into stirrups, not for climbing up a mountainside.

Gene Adams was first to clamber to his feet and stare down to their right where the river rushed. The blue sky edged the water as it flowed steadily over the waterfall and crashed down to the valley below.

'Come with me, Johnny,' Adams said to the youngster.

'What about me, Gene?' Tomahawk

asked as he scratched his head. 'What'll I do?'

'Tie up the horses and give them grain,' Adams answered as the young man got to his feet and stood beside him.

'Where are we going?' Johnny Puma wondered aloud.

'We are going to take a look over the edge of the fall.' Adams was smiling. 'Just to see who was hiding down there.'

'What if there ain't nobody down there, Gene?'

'Then we have wasted a lot of time and energy for nothing, son.' Gene Adams led the way with the young cowboy directly behind him.

As both men moved through the dense undergrowth they soon became aware that no other creatures had ever been to where they were heading. Every inch that they proceeded tore at their clothing. This was the most painful of trips that either man had ever undertaken. Inch by inch they edged closer to the rim of the over-hanging cliff next to

·the fast-flowing river as it roared off and down at suicidal speed.

Adams leaned on his elbows as the younger man moved beside him and stared down. At first they saw nothing unusual. Then as they waited they noticed that the scene below was not quite as normal as they had first thought.

The ground near the pool between the overgrown area was torn up since the recent rain. Someone had tried to brush away the evidence but the sodden soil still bore the marks of activity when gazed down upon from a great height.

'What do you reckon, Johnny?' Adams asked.

Johnny Puma sighed as he leaned over the steep dangerous ciff. 'Looks odd to me.'

'Me too,' Adams agreed.

'Something happened down there since the rain.'

'Just what I was thinking.' Adams strained his eyes trying to see what was going on below. 'The rain would have washed away all signs of our herd and left the ground pretty flat and level.'

Johnny looked up at the sky above their heads. The black buzzards circled as if frightened to land. He nudged Adams's arm with his elbow and nodded at the birds.

'They know something.'

'So do I.' Gene Adams smiled as he drew himself up on to his wrists to gain a better look.

Johnny followed the direction of Adams's gloved finger with his eyes and soon focused on the moving bushes far below them.

'Who is that, Gene?'

'I figure whoever it is, is waiting for us.' Adams gave Johnny a glance.

Johnny chewed his lip. 'They're after the Bar 10 gold.'

Adams looked again. 'You're right. There are two critters down there ready to bushwhack us on our way home.'

'What we gonna do, Gene?' Johnny knew that they had to do something.

'The first thing we do is make camp

and get some grub in our bellies.'

'What's the second thing we do, Gene?'

Adams rested on his side staring at his partner. 'Then when we have had some food and a cup of old Tomahawk's coffee, we get the ropes off our saddles and shimmy down over this ledge.'

Johnny stared down at the drop. It was wet with the incessant spray off the waterfall.

Their eyes met. Johnny Puma knew that Gene Lon Adams was serious. Deadly serious.

11

Night came with all its usual luggage. Stars, moonlight and cold breezes that found their way into every bone of the trio of cowboys. Gene Adams knew his plan was ambitious and had silently prayed that his younger friend might come up with something less dangerous. They had eaten and made temporary camp and the plan to climb down the cliff next to the falls was still the only one that was being considered. At least they had felt comfortable enough to light a roaring fire that reached into the heavens above. Gene Adams knew that this blaze could not be seen by the bushwhackers far below near the pool as he toyed with his tin cup and the last of his coffee. Tomahawk lifted another bundle of kindling and dropped it into the centre of the flames. At long last the heat was beginning to resonate around the three bedrolls as the men finished off the coffee.

Somehow both Adams and Johnny Puma knew that they had one hell of a night ahead of them. A night when blood might be shed for no good reason. A night when they would have to climb down their saddle ropes until they reached the foot of the waterfall and then, if they were still able, face the men who were hiding in the undergrowth around the pool. Neither Puma nor Adams were keen on the idea of going over the edge of the cliff behind them but during their meal of fried beans they had not thought of a better idea. Both the younger men watched each other silently, knowing that they could no longer delay the moment of truth.

Gene Adams got carefully to his feet and moved across the lush area that skirted the river, towards their unsaddled horses which were tied to thin saplings. He leaned over, knelt down and untied his curled rope from the horn of his saddle. He then untied Johnny's rope before standing to his full height. For a moment he watched the moonlight dancing off the fast-flowing river near them. His thoughts were troubled as he gripped the ropes firmly in each of his gloved hands.

Tomahawk and the young man watched as the silent rancher walked back towards them carrying the ropes with narrow focused eyes that seemed to burn into them. Neither Johnny nor Gene had spoken during their meal as both pondered upon the rancher's idea. Even though the sharp breeze chilled the evening air, sweat ran down both their faces as they watched the old-timer obliviously scratching his bread.

'What you want with them ropes, Gene?' Tomahawk asked as the tall man stopped above him.

Adams tossed one rope to Johnny. 'Me and the boy are going for a little jaunt.'

'What's a jaunt?' the old-timer asked.

'We are going to climb down next to the waterfall,' Johnny answered quietly.

Tomahawk started to laugh. 'What you really gonna do with them ropes?'

'We are gonna use the ropes to hold on to, you old fool.' Adams shook his head.

'Sort of like a couple of monkeys?' Johnny said as his eyes and fingers checked the condition of his rope.

Gene Adams smiled at the old man. It was a smile that said more than any words could. Suddenly Tomahawk knew that he had been told the truth and gasped.

'You crazy?' he squealed like a stuck pig. 'You are too old to go hanging on ropes, Gene.'

'I ain't that old.'

'Look at your hair. It's been snowing up there for the longest time, Gene.' Tomahawk shook his head in a mixture of worry and annoyance that he was no longer able to do such stupid things.

'There might be snow on my roof but the fire's still lit.' Gene Adams started to test his rope for strength.

'Yep,' Johnny replied as he reluctantly got off the ground and dusted himself off. 'We are real crazy.'

'You got a better idea, Tomahawk?' Gene Adams pulled the draw-string of his ten-gallon hat tight under his chin. 'Because I'm open to any suggestions.'

Tomahawk's face went blank as he clambered to his feet and stood between his two friends. There was one thing he was not very good at, and that was coming up with plans.

'I thought not.' Adams gave the old man a pat on the back.

'So what exactly are you boys thinking of doing?' Tomahawk's entire body seemed to quiver as he spoke.

Johnny watched as Adams squared up to them both and outlined his plans.

'First me and Johnny shimmy down the ropes to the edge of the pool,' he explained, staring directly into Tomahawk's eyes. 'Then when we are down, you pull up the ropes and put them back on our saddles. Then you lead our horses back down the trail through the woods until you reach the flat plain where we started.

'What'll you boys be doing?' Tomahawk raised his long white eyebrows as he asked the question.

'We'll be trying to find out who exactly is hiding down there in the bushes next to the water-hole.' Adams started to move towards the ridge when Tomahawk's skinny old hand grabbed the sleeve of his coat. 'I figure that we might end up in a bit of gunplay. You head for the water-hole with our horses when you hear the shooting end.'

'What if you boys get yourselves killed by them varmints?'

'Then ride quietly with your gun handy.' Gene could not help smiling at the bewildered old man. 'When you get close to the pool you better whistle.'

Tomahawk's face seemed to crunch up. 'You know I ain't got enough teeth left to whistle.'

'Stop worrying.' Adams gave a reassuring smile to the old man.

'You take care, Gene,' Tomahawk said quietly. 'I'm just getting used to you.'

Adams started to chuckle. 'I always take care.'

'What about me?' Johnny asked holding on to his rope.

'You is so young I can't see why you need the rope.' The old man sniffed as he followed the two men up the slope to the cliff edge next to the fast flowing river. 'You could just hop down there like a jackass rabbit.'

The three men stared down into the darkness where only the moonlight penetrated. It was like looking into a bottomless pit and only the sound of the waterfall gave them some clue as to how far they would have to climb. Gene Adams secured the safety loops over the hammers of his gold-plated guns and watched as his young friend did the same. The last thing either of these two cowboys wanted was to have their weapons falling from their holsters as they made their descent.

'Put your gloves on, Johnny,' Adams

ordered. 'You don't want rope burns on your trigger fingers.'

The youngster reached into his pockets and put on his gloves before looking at the two men. 'You ready, Gene?'

'Nope,' Adams said as he dropped the rope down into the darkness before tying the end to a stout tree trunk.

'Me neither,' the young man sighed as he followed suit with his rope.

'Are them ropes long enough, Gene?' Tomahawk stared at the silver-haired man.

'I sure hope so, old man.' Adams wrapped his rope around his wide back and stepped over the edge with it gripped firmly in his gloved hands. It was like leaning over nothing at all as he carefully took the strain of the tight rope and started to move backwards into the darkness.

'Me too,' Johnny Puma laughed as he backed over the cliff carefully. The sweat ran down his young face belying his devil-may-care attitude. As he focused upon the rope in his hands and braced his feet against the wet cliff face, he went suddenly very silent. This was not something he could remember ever doing before, and he promised himself that he would never do it ever again.

Soon both of the cowboys disappeared from Tomahawk's view. He watched the blackness and the two vibrating twitching ropes. As long as the ropes remained taut, the old-timer knew his friends were still holding on to them. He waited on his knees for the ropes to go slack so that he could haul them back up and do as he had been ordered by Adams. It seemed a simple plan but that made him nervous. Very nervous indeed.

12

The thunderous roaring of the water falling past them as they slowly descended the cliff face was deafening, mind-splitting. The continuous spray made everything exceedingly wet, including the two cowboys, as they edged their way slowly down into the darkness. The ropes were becoming dangerously slippery in their gloved hands and they soon discovered that moss covered every inch of the cliff face under their Cuban heels. They seemed to swing from side to side as their boots lost contact with the soaking surface of the cliff face. The power of the water as it roared past them made them feel like marionettes in the hands of a puppeteer who had drunk too many bottles of redeye. The descent was becoming more and more hazardous, as for every yard they managed to climb down their ropes they ran five or six feet to either side of their chosen direction.

The descent was taking far longer than either man had anticipated as they fought feverishly to remain in control of the wet, greasy, grass-fibre ropes. The wetter the ropes got, the more they stretched and became harder to grip. The younger man was amazed that his companion was managing to keep alongside him. The incredible strength that both men were exerting was testament to the fact that they, like all the cowboys on the Bar 10 Ranch, were used to fighting with ropes. Usually it was a cantankerous steer that tried to rip their arms from their sockets during round-up, but this was far worse.

Gene Adams knew that they had to get down to ground level as fast as possible but also realized that there was no way that either of them could risk rushing their descent.

Every passing second seemed to last hours as Johnny Puma and Gene Adams plunged ever downward into the blackness. The ropes became more and more impossible to grip and they suddenly found themselves sliding downward next to one another. Down into the blackness. Neither cowboy made a sound as they plunged down unable to grasp the ropes tight enough to stop their fall into the unknown. Terror filled both men's breasts as they felt their speed increasing as the ropes sped through their gloved hands.

Then, suddenly, both cowboys found their boots hitting the wet mud together. They tumbled head over heels into the wet soft mud. They thanked the Lord that whatever noise they had made was drowned in the constant sound of the waterfall beside them. Slowly, they both clambered unsteadily to their feet and looked around desperately, trying to gather their bearings. It was Gene Adams who was first to work out exactly where they were amid the mud. The glance from Adams to his young friend as they released their ropes indicated which direction they would take. Before either man had moved away from the soaking rock face the ropes started to be slowly hauled up by Tomahawk far above them. Johnny trailed the older man into the bushes as they found their way into the thick lush foliage that surrounded the pool. The walk around the edge of the wide pool seemed to take hours as both the cowboys had to forge their way through tall reeds and immature trees as well as the soft damp ground that tried its best to suck off their high-heeled boots. They were totally exhausted by the time they had reached the opposite side of the pool from where they had landed at the foot of the falls. They were just two hundred yards away from the waterfall when Gene Adams silently raised his right arm to his partner. Both men stopped.

Johnny Puma moved alongside Adams and squinted at what he was pointing at. Two men were crouching in the undergrowth thirty feet before them. Adams leaned over and whispered in Johnny's ear. The two men were both recognizable to the cowboys from the Bar 10.

'Ain't that our old friend Mr Chargon?'

'Yep, and ain't that Fred Smith the cattle buyer with him?' Johnny hardly believed his eyes. It was dark but not that dark.

'You're right.' Adams blew out a sigh of disbelief. It seemed impossible that these two characters would know each other let alone be involved together in this sort of business. Something caught the older cowboy's attention as he silently sniffed the air around them. It was the putrid smell of death that drifted up and filled both their nostrils as they paused watching the two bushwhackers.

'You smell that, Johnny?' Adams whispered.

Johnny nodded. 'What is it?'

Adams held his breath and moved

past his young friend. He pushed some tall brush away before seeing the three bodies piled up. The stench was overwhelming.

'Who are they?' Johnny asked quietly over Adams's shoulder.

'Dead folks.' Adams turned and returned to where they had a perfect view of the two men ahead of them. 'I guess they got here when Smith and Chargon were expecting us.'

'Do you reckon Chargon killed them?' Johnny asked naïvely.

'Seems a reasonable assumption, Johnny.' Gene Adams flicked off the hammer loops before drawing both his golden Colt forty-fives. 'That was meant to be us, I reckon.'

'Who do you reckon they were, Gene?' Johnny wondered as he thought about the three innocent victims.

'They might be some of our wranglers heading home,' Gene muttered in a low thoughtful voice. 'Whoever they were, they didn't deserve to end up like that.'

'So that's why we spotted them buzzards circling.'

'Those birds can smell a carcass even if it's buried.' Gene Adams knew that whatever else they faced this long night, they couldn't rule out ending up the same as the bodies that were piled up in the undergrowth. It had been a very long time since they had used their weapons in anger and that was worrying the rancher. 'And those bodies are pretty ripe.'

'I ain't never had nothing smell that bad get up my nose before, Gene.' The young cowhand rubbed his face trying to rid his senses of the aroma that had filled his nostrils.

'Get your irons out,' Adams said through gritted teeth.

Johnny Puma did as he was instructed and drew both his pistols. Now both men were primed for action.

'You ready?' Gene Adams asked.

'Yep. I'm ready.'

13

'How we gonna do this?' Johnny Puma asked as they stood watching the two men ahead of them through the bushes and thick undergrowth.

'Head on,' Gene Adams grunted in a low firm tone. 'I like to face my enemies head on.'

It was still mighty dark around the waterhole beneath the falls. Only moonlight gave them any idea of what was ahead of them as they stood preparing to advance upon the bush-whackers.

'Gene?' the young voice said, 'I just thought of something that maybe you might have overlooked.'

Gene Adams turned and stared into the shadowy face beside him in the bushes. 'What?'

'Maybe there are more than just Chargon and Smith hiding out there.'

Johnny rested his arm on the wide shoulder of the older man. 'We might be looking at taking on a half-dozen varmints when we are only expecting the two.'

Adams thought deeply for a few moments before nodding in agreement. It was true, he had assumed that there were only the two gunmen lying in wait for them. There might be more. An awful lot more that they just could not see in the darkness of night. He stood motionless for several moments looking around the scene before speaking.

'You ready to toss a few stones, Johnny?' Gene Adams had a smile on his face as he spoke. It was a smile that reassured the young cowboy.

'What?' Johnny Puma stood with a puzzled expression on his face.

Gene Adams holstered one of his guns and then knelt down and picked up a few large stones. He handed a couple to Johnny and leaned closer to whisper.

'You throw your stones that way and

I'll throw mine this way and we'll see what happens.' Adams watched as Johnny Puma started to grin at the idea. 'We might be able to figure out if them critters are alone or have company.'

The two men from the Bar 10 threw the stones at exactly the same time in opposite directions. Johnny's landed out beyond the trees that led to the pool and its cold fresh water, whilst Adams's stones splashed loudly into the water. With guns gripped firmly in their hands they watched as both Chargon and Fred C. Smith rose from the bushes with their weapons ready to kill. The trick had worked, and both the would-be bushwhackers did not have any idea where to look or aim their guns.

'Drop those guns, boys,' Adams ordered stepping out from the bushes holding his two golden guns in his hands. Johnny Puma was at his side.

Smith froze as he suddenly became aware of the two men walking towards them in the moonlight. Chargon stood grinning over his friend's shoulder. He had no intention of listening to anyone, let alone the man with the golden-plated Colt forty-fives.

'I said drop them guns,' Adams reiterated loudly.

Smith gave Chargon a frantic glance. 'What are we gonna do, Chargon?'

'Shoot it out, Mr Smith,' Chargon smiled. 'We are gonna shoot it out.'

Before the small New Yorker could say another word, his tall companion raised his pistol and started shooting over his head at Adams and Puma.

Gene Adams was never a man to run away from a fight and this was a fight. He fell on to one knee and started to return the fire into the direction of the bushwhackers. The brilliant flashes of charged powder as it sent bullets flying across the clearing lit up the dark scene making the figures appear like phantoms.

Lead and fire filled the air as both pairs of men started emptying their weapons at each other. After firing both his forty-fives in the general direction of the enemy, Johnny Puma made a move to his left as a bullet hit his shoulder, forcing him to drop one of his guns as he crumpled into the mud behind the kneeling Adams. The young man raised his remaining weapon and squeezed the trigger, sending one final bullet into the bushes that sheltered Smith and Chargon before he felt everything going dark inside his head.

Gene Adams knew that his friend was hurt very badly as he continued firing at the two men opposite through the smoke that the guns were discharging. He then rolled over to get a better view from beneath the gunsmoke before seeing Smith taking aim at Johnny where he lay nursing his wound. Without a second's hesitation, Adams aimed his left-hand Colt at the small man and fired.

As Fred C. Smith fell backward, Gene Adams knew instinctively that the evil little man was dead. Then using the smokescreen as cover he crawled forward after Chargon.

The tall man was now packing not only his own pistol but Smith's as well as he moved through the undergrowth seeking cover in the darkness.

Gene Adams got to his feet and entered the bushes, stepping over Smith's lifeless body as he pursued the gunman. A bullet passed by over the rancher's head like a firefly, causing him to duck as he moved onward after his prey. For all he knew, Johnny was dead where he lay and this alone gave him the courage to keep heading on after the vermin named Chargon.

Adams raised both his guns and searched the scene for a clue as to which direction the tall man had fled. Then another bullet came at him and spliced a sapling in half next to his head.

That was all he wanted. A rough idea of which direction to send his hot lead. Getting to his feet, he held both his gleaming pistols together and pulled both triggers several times until no more bullets came out of his barrels. Holstering one gun he quickly reloaded the other before moving forward again. The gold-plated Colt was heavier than most guns but his hands were used to the extra weight and used it to good advantage. Like a hound on a coon hunt, Gene Adams followed the trail left by the tall ruthless back-shooter. He could smell the fear leaving the man's body as he backed off away from the rancher. Then he saw the moonlight catching the back of Chargon's torso thirty feet ahead of him.

'Give it up, Chargon,' Adams screamed furiously at the man.

'Like hell I will,' Chargon yelled back, raising his guns and firing at the approaching rancher. Each bullet seemed to pass so close to Adams's face that he felt his skin burning with the heat of thir venom. 'Come on, Adams. Come and eat my lead.'

'Give it up,' Adams shouted once more.

'Swallow this, Mister Bar 10.' Chargon pulled hard on his triggers once again.

Then as if in a trance, Gene Adams lifted his fully charged golden forty-five and fired one shell in return. It was the one shell that ended the battle. Adams's hooded blue eyes watched as the evil Chargon dropped on to his knees and fell face down into the mud.

The rancher checked the body briefly before returning to the clearing at breakneck speed. The sight that met his eyes through the still thick gunsmoke made his steps falter. It was the sight that he knew he would see. The sight of Johnny Puma lying where he had fallen. It was a sight that filled the rancher with total horror.

Gene Adams moved slowly towards the prostrate figure as it lay in the mud, still clutching one of the pistols. The youngster was motionless as the mature cowboy knelt down beside him, afraid of what he might find when he eventually turned him over.

All that Adams could see was the blood around his young friend and he felt his guts churn as he somehow managed to touch Johnny's still frame.

The sound of the cowboy groaning as he was turned over made Gene Adams heave a huge sigh of relief.

'Johnny,' he croaked.

'Get me on my feet, Gene.' The youngster spat the mud out of his mouth.

'Will do, partner.' Adams sighed as his heart once again started to beat at its normal rate.

14

It was almost dawn when Tomahawk rounded the edge of the clearing with his two friends' horses in tow. He reined in hard as he saw the two men on the ground beside a lot of dried blood. Without hesitation the old-timer dropped off his black horse and rushed forward.

His old eyes studied Johnny Puma's shoulder wound which Gene Adams was pressing hard with his gloved left hand.

'It's about time you got here,' Adams snapped.

'I'm sorry but it ain't easy pulling two nags along down that trail,' Tomahawk replied as he knelt beside the wounded youngster. He pulled up one of Johnny's eyelids and then released his grip. 'How long he been out, Gene?'

'It must be an hour,' Adams sighed.

'I'll make a fire,' Tomahawk said getting to his feet.

'What?'

'I gotta cut that slug out of there,' the old man sighed.

Adams held on to the young man firmly. 'Hurry up. He's lost a lot of blood.'

Tomahawk had a camp-fire blazing within ten minutes and sat watching the long knife as it rested in the flames.

'You sure you can do this, Tomahawk?' Gene Adams asked with concern in his voice.

Tomahawk raised his white brows. 'I gotta get it out and then burn the hole to stop the bleeding.'

Adams hugged the youngster as he watched Tomahawk checking the hot blade of his knife. If this went wrong, he thought, could he ever forgive himself for dragging the kid into this fight?

'Pull his shirt away from the wound, Gene,' Tomahawk instructed as he hovered with the knife in his hand.

For once, Gene Adams was the one taking orders. For once he was glad he was not the one having to dig around in Johnny's shoulder looking for an ounce of lead.

With an almost expert precision, Tomahawk managed to locate the bullet and dig it out from the wound quickly. He forced the blade into the flames once more and then pulled it out and rested its smoking edge upon the bleeding skin. The skin was sealed by flame.

'Is that it?' Gene Adams was shocked at how fast the old man had worked and completed his task. 'You done?'

'I'm finished,' Tomahawk said as he got to his feet and leaned on his saddle.

Gene Adams rested the young man down on the ground. 'Get me my bedroll to put under his head, Toma-hawk.'

Tomahawk gave a sigh and moved to the chestnut mare. He dragged the heavy saddle-bags off the horse's hindquarters, dropping them on to the ground. As he pulled off the bedroll he spotted something. Something not quite right.

'Come on, bring me that bedroll,' Adams called impatiently.

Tomahawk watched the ground as he threw the bedroll to his boss. 'You ain't gonna like this, Gene.'

Adams tucked the bedroll under the head of the sleeping Johnny Puma and got to his feet. 'What did you say?'

Tomahawk looked across at him. 'I said that you ain't gonna like this.'

'What do you mean?' Adams walked towards Tomahawk and then saw what the old man was talking about.

At their feet, the saddle-bag had split open and on the ground lay lead and steel washers.

'Ain't this supposed to be gold, Gene?' Tomahawk scratched his beard as he watched his friend move to Johnny's pinto and drag off the other saddle-bag. That was also filled with lead and steel hardware.

'Where's our gold?' Adams said with a puzzled look on his face.

'We ain't got it. That's for sure.' Tomahawk sniffed noisily. 'Should I make us some coffee?'

Gene Adams stared at their young friend lying on the ground then at the worthless washers. 'Make us some breakfast too,' he said quietly, trying to figure out where their money had gone. 'We gotta wait until the boy wakes up before we can go anywhere.'

'Where you figure we ought to go?' Tomahawk asked as he pulled off his bags from the back of his black gelding and started to pull out the pan and grub.

'Back to Sutters Corner,' Adams replied.

'Why there?' The old man knelt down and placed the pan upon the fire.

Adams did not reply. He had no answers left, only a lot of questions.

15

It was early afternoon when the three riders pulled their mounts up before the old hotel at Sutters Corner. The long ride from the falls had taken far longer than usual as Adams and Tomahawk had to ride with the wounded Johnny Puma between them. For most of the journey the youngster had drifted in and out of consciousness and would have fallen between his outriders were it not for their observance. Tomahawk was first off his black gelding and held on to Johnny Puma as he carefully dismounted from the pinto. The young man was still incredibly weak and had been curled up in pain since waking up back at the falls. Gene Adams reined in his chestnut and watched as the two men slowly ascended the wooden steps to the porch of the hotel. Then he looked down the deserted street of broken buildings: all that remained of many people's great dreams. The sun beat down mercilessly upon the bleached buildings as a thought crept into his fertile mind.

Adams could not ignore the question that had drifted into his thoughts. The only way to find an answer was to go back to the scene of the shooting, the jailhouse. Adams spurred his mount and galloped down the ghost town's long main street. Getting to the old jailhouse he quickly dismounted and moved around the area once again as he had done the previous day.

Once again, there was nothing to see. Nothing except the tracks that led up the alleyway to the rear of the ramshackle buildings. Without knowing exactly why Adams followed the tracks. There was something gnawing at his craw yet he had no idea what it was. All he knew for certain was that if there was an answer, this was where he might find it.

Ignoring his own boot-prints, as well

as those of his two trusty friends, he eventually started to make out the marks left by the man who had opened up on them with a Winchester.

When he got to the point where the mysterious rifleman had ridden away, he knelt and studied the tracks with a keen eye for clues that might have eluded him when he was last at this point.

What he had failed to do the previous day was take in the signs that were there for any experienced tracker to see. How he could not have noticed the clues in the soft sand made the rancher angry with his own stupidity. He was kneeling down examining the ground when Tomahawk came running up behind him. It was like being approached by a hairy sidewinder.

'What you playing at, Gene?' the old man puffed as he finally came to a stop.

'These tracks.' Adams waved his arm over the undisturbed scene. 'They're screaming out at me but I ain't as keen a tracker as you are.'

'Git out the way, boy,' Tomahawk moved closer. 'Let an expert see the apple-pie.' He knelt down beside Adams.

'What you make of these tracks, old-timer?' asked Adams.

'Horseshoe tracks.'

'Brilliant.' Adams shook his head. 'I'd figured that much myself. Anything else?'

'High-heel boot-prints.' Tomahawk pointed. 'This is where the guy with the carbine mounted and lit out after shooting at us.'

'Anything else?'

'Yep. I know these tracks.' Tomahawk started to grin in his own amazing way.

'You recognize them?' Adams knelt upright, then leaned forward to where the old man was pointing. 'Who do they belong to, Tomahawk?'

'That I ain't certain of.' Tomahawk rubbed his beard. 'But it was someone on our trail drive. I seen these tracks a few times around the chuck-wagon at grub times.

'How can you tell?'

Tomahawk pointed at the boot prints in the sand. 'See that left boot? It has a real worn heel and a split across the sole.'

'So it has.' Adams patted the old man on the back.

'See the horseshoe tracks? One of the shoes has a small bit missing off it.' Tomahawk nodded to himself. It was like a novel written in the sand for someone like him to read. The old man had never mastered reading words but little else got past his experienced eyes. He had spent too many years during his youth up in the high country with the Kiowa learning how to survive off the land.

Both men rose to their feet and dusted themselves off. The tall rancher ran his gloved fingers along his chin thinking hard as they walked back along the narrow alley to the waiting chestnut mare.

'What you thinking about, Gene?' Tomahawk asked as the rancher brooded on his thoughts in the burning hot sunshine.

'One of our men off the trail drive was rooting around in the jailhouse real loudly,' Adams mused, pointing to the ruined structure. 'In itself, that don't make any sense.'

'Strange.' Tomahawk nodded as they reached the mare. 'Makes no sense. No sense at all. The varmint almost seemed to want us to hear him.'

'You hit the nail on the head.' Adams smiled.

'What nail?' Tomahawk was confused by the metaphor.

'Let's go back to the hotel and check around the building.'

'What for, Gene?' Tomahawk walked beside the rancher as he led the tall chestnut back up the street towards the hotel.

'I think we ought to check,' Adams said in a low voice as they paced up the deserted street.

'For what?'

'The other man's tracks,' Adams

answered, giving the old-timer a glance. 'The man with the rifle was making a lot of noise to distract us away from the hotel. That's all he was, a distraction. A diversion to keep us occupied. He did his job well and think about it, we were away for nearly a quarter of an hour.'

'So that the other guy . . . ' Tomahawk found his sentence being finished by the rancher.

'Exactly. So the other man could sneak into the hotel and go to our room and steal our gold, replacing it with lead and steel scrap metal.' At the hotel Adams stopped and moved to the side of the building where he soon found the churned up ground he was seeking.

'Where did he get all the junk from to fill our saddle-bags with, Gene?' The old-timer scratched his beard as he spoke.

'From the old blacksmith's down the road.' Gene pointed over his shoulder. 'The place must be full of junk. Nice heavy junk which is almost exactly the same weight as our gold.'

Tomahawk pointed at the scene before them. 'This is where the varmint tied up his horse and entered the hotel by breaking into this window.'

Gene Adams ran a gloved hand over the damaged woodwork of the window at the side of the hotel, before agreeing with his friend. 'Pretty smart.'

'What ya mean?'

'We might not have found out about the switch until we arrived back on the Bar 10, Tomahawk.' Adams chewed his lower lip as he thought aloud. 'In a way, Chargon and Smith did us a favour by trying to bushwhack us. Oherwise we might never have found out that our money had turned into scrap metal.'

'Now what?' Tomahawk asked as Adams tied his chestnut mare up to the hitching rail next to the pinto and the gelding.

Adams climbed up the wooden steps towards the hotel entrance with Tomahawk on his heels. Just before they were about to enter, he placed a hand upon the old-timer's shoulder and stared into his wrinkled old face.

'First we make sure young Johnny is OK,' Adams smiled at the ground. 'Then we head back to McCoy.'

'Why McCoy?'

'Where else would they go?' Adams gave a heavy sigh as he felt suddenly refreshed by the knowledge that they had just acquired. 'Two saddle-bags full of gold coin are mighty heavy. Whoever has got them bags has got to find a way of getting out of McCoy.'

'What d'you mean?' Tomahawk raised his eyebrows.

'I figure they'll try to get on the next train north.' Adams smiled.

'Why would they wanna catch a train?'

'Because a man with a saddle-bag full of gold on a horse can be easily caught by someone without a heavy saddle-bag of gold on his horse, Tomahawk.' Adams looked into the dark cool hotel and to the beautiful Nancy Davis as she hovered over Johnny in the lobby. 'A train lets them flee in style.'

'So when is the next train out of McCoy?'

Gene Adams gave another smile and gently tugged his friend's beard. 'Midnight.'

16

It was 6.30 in the evening by the time Gene Adams and his faithful friend Tomahawk rode into the sprawling cattle town on their sweating mounts. They had made good time and ridden hard and long to arrive so soon after sunset.

The men rode slowly down the long street next to the rail tracks which was made up of nothing more than one cattle pen after another. Two thirds of the pens were occupied with Adams's prime beef on the hoof, waiting to be loaded on the train when it arrived. The darkness was lit with street lamps which burned their coal oil brightly around the scene. The moon above seemed fainter now as the glowing orange lamplights sent their light into the heavens as well as to the ground.

Neither rider seemed to notice the

sudden drop in temperature as they rode quietly along the steel rails that headed closer and closer to the buildings edging the heart of the cattle town.

McCoy was an eerie place after dark. It took on a sinister atmosphere that could not be described, only experienced. There was many a soul who never appeared during daylight hours, only emerging to haunt the numerous saloons whilst the street lights glowed.

This was a town on the edge of civilization which had to be there to supply the butchers' shops back East. Trouble was, the law had not caught up with the railhead. It had tried but there were just too many guns in this town. Too much money was being made by the wrong sorts. Adams knew this town and had seen it grow from nothing in the prairie. Now, he had doubts about the shadows and those who dwelled in their darkness.

Here only the gun seemed to rule.

Especially after the sun set and the street lights were lit.

Gene Adams rode tall in his saddle as he moved his tired mare between the pens. Tomahawk seemed to melt into his saddle and moved along with only one hand upon the reins whilst the other rested upon the Indian hatchet whose name he bore.

The two men never stopped watching everyone and everything that caught their attention. As they turned into the main street of the cattle town, their horses were startled for a brief second. The teeming crowds that seemed to flow from one street bar to the next made the prospect of finding the two men who had stolen their gold a daunting one.

Tomahawk drew his horse close to his friend's and looked up at him as they steered the two creatures along the crowded way.

'What's the matter, old friend?' Adams asked without looking at his pal. 'You seem troubled.'

'This is going to be tough.' Tomahawk spat at the ground as his old eyes watched every person and animal that crossed their paths as they rode.

'Yep.' Adams smiled.

Tomahawk gave a slight laugh as he followed the tall chestnut up to the saloon hitching rail. This was the drinking-hole that they had been in when they had paid off the trail crew. If it had a name, neither man knew it. They dismounted and tied the reins tightly to the rail before entering through the swing doors.

'We might see a few familiar faces,' Adams said as their bodies cut through the smoke that hung at five feet across the wide room. Every table was being used and there had to be over a thousand playing cards in action as they carved their way to the long bar.

'You see anyone we knows?' Tomahawk asked as the palm of his hand rested on the head of his stone axe.

'Not yet.' Adams leaned on the bar and tipped his ten-gallon hat back on his head. The mirror behind the busy bartenders was blurred with cigarette and cigar smoke as the two cowboys used its reflections to see along the entire length of the wooden structure. Every face seemed alien to them as their tired eyes searched the reflected images.

Turning to face the entire room full of folks made both men suddenly realize how many souls were within the four walls of the saloon.

'See any of our boys?' Adams asked his partner.

'Not yet, Gene.'

'What'll it be?' A barman's voice piped up behind them.

Adams turned and smiled at the man. 'Seen any of my trail hands tonight?'

'Who are you, fella?' the man asked, staring at the rancher with eyes that failed to recognize someone he had served many times over the years.

'Forget it,' Adams said, pulling his hat down over his eyes and turning away from the barman.

'I ain't seen any of our boys,' Tomahawk sniffed, rubbing his nose on his sleeve.

'Me neither,' Adams sighed, with disappointment written across his face. He shrugged and left the bar with Tomahawk at his side. They did not stop walking until they had entered the next saloon.

'What do you think?' Tomahawk asked as they faced yet another crowded room.

'I'm starting to get worried,' Adams confessed. 'I never figured there were so many people in this damn town.'

The two men drifted through the saloon and paid attention to every face that their trail-weary eyes spied. Then they saw the one face that neither had expected, sitting behind a well-used bottle of rye.

'Cookie,' Adams said in a voice that boomed over the head of the ill-tempered man as they dragged out two chairs and seated themselves. The green-topped table was stained beyond any hope of salvation as Tomahawk and Adams rested their elbows and stared into the face of their trail cook.

'What you critters want with me?' the cook snarled in his usual tone.

'We were just looking for a friendly face,' Adams lied.

'Then beat it and find one,' the cook grunted, pouring another drink into his glass tumbler before swilling it down in one.

It seemed curious to Adams that this man had not asked what they were doing back in town when all the trail crew knew that they had headed back for the Bar 10 two days earlier.

'You heading home soon?' Adams asked as he stroked the table with his gloved hands.

'What's it got to do with you, Adams?' Cookie stared at the men opposite him with something like hatred in his face.

'Nothing I guess.' Adams sat upright

and tipped his hat off his brow. 'You seen any of the other hands tonight?'

'Nope.' Cookie's reply almost preceded the question in its sharpness and speed off his tongue.

Tomahawk rubbed his dry mouth. 'Can I have a swig, Cookie?'

'Buy your own liquor, old man.'

Gene Adams could not understand why any man would choose to go through life with anger, it always seemed such a negative state to be in. 'You angry with me and Tomahawk?'

'Nope.'

'Then why the poison?'

'I hate rich folks.' Cookie grinned, an expression that was not meant to display humour, only displeasure.

Adams nodded. He accepted the drunken reasons that were being thrown at him. 'So you ain't seen any of our boys off the drive tonight?'

'That is correct.' Cookie made a face as he poured yet another shot of whiskey into his glass. 'Even if I had do you think I'd tell you?'

'Nope. I guess not.' Adams gave a regretful sigh.

'Now let me alone. I don't work for you any more.' Cookie had been the most bitter man ever to work the chuck-wagon on any of Adams's trail drives. His glassy stare did little to encourage the rancher from the Bar 10 to employ him in the future.

'What was your real name again, Cookie?' Adams glared.

'Robert Bates.' Cookie grinned again. 'Why?'

'I just wanna make sure I never hire you on again.'

Cookie gave a chuckle that indicated that he didn't give a damn. All he was concerned with was his tall bottle of rye.

Adams got to his feet and gestured for Tomahawk to do the same. 'You've been very helpful, Cookie.'

Cookie gazed up at the pair with a twisted smile on his cracked lips. 'You lost something, Mr Adams?'

Adams hesitated for a moment before

turning away from the man. As both he and Tomahawk made their way out of the busy saloon he muttered under his breath.

'What you say, Gene?' the old-timer asked.

'I just wondered if Cookie might know something he ought not to know, Tomahawk,' Adams sighed. 'Like the fact that some son of a bitch has our gold.'

'Then why not ask him?'

'Maybe later.'

Standing on the boardwalk amid the ceaselessly moving people of McCoy made both men pensive.

'What you thinking about, old-timer?' Adams asked as he rested his hands on the handles of his golden guns.

'Livery stable.' Tomahawk smiled.

Adams gave a smile in return. 'Good thinking. Maybe that horse with the broken shoe is in the livery stable.'

'I figured that if you was right about the thief catching a train out of here, he'd have to sell his horse.' Tomahawk was trying hard not to allow the swelling in his chest move to his head.

'Not a bad assumption.' Gene Adams chewed his lower lip as he moved towards their horses.

'I ain't just a pretty face, am I?' Tomahawk beamed.

'Not hardly.' Adams slapped the old man hard on his back. 'No man could ever say you was just a pretty face.'

The two men forced their way back to their horses through the teeming crowd and mounted. Riding fast down the long street to the main livery they weaved their way around all the obstacles before them. Two streets away they caught sight of the large stables. This street was quieter than the main streets around the drinking and gambling palaces.

The two men pulled up hard and stared at the large locked doors that confronted them.

'Locked?' Tomahawk jumped off his gelding and tried in vain to force the large doors. His eyes wrinkled up as he stared at his friend sitting motionless in the saddle.

'That is the first time I ever seen a livery stable locked up to the public,' Adams said quietly, staring up at the tall building. His eyes focused upon the square opening over the main doors with a rope and pulley above it. He knew that was where the hay was stored.

'Reckon you could get up there, old-timer?' Adams asked. His tongue was firmly in his cheek as he watched the whiskers ruffle around the mouth with so few remaining teeth.

Tomahawk stared up at the dangling rope. 'Twenty years ago.'

'Thirty years ago,' Adam laughed. 'Come and hold my horse steady. I'll give it a try.'

The old man held the head of the chestnut mare steady as he watched Adams carefully climb on to his saddle and balance for a few seconds. He reached up and caught hold of the rope that hung from the pulley and gave it a tug to check that it was tied to something solid. It was fixed securely to a broad pine beam inside the hay loft of the livery and was capable of taking his weight easily.

Adams hauled himself up into the air and soon reached the pulley itself, swinging across the gap then, using his long legs to grab the wall, he cautiously entered the high loft.

Tomahawk stood watching, open-mouthed, as his friend disappeared inside the dark building through the loft. A few moments later he heard the sound of bolts being released and the doors being pushed open. It was an exhausted Gene Adams who stood before the old man, shaking his head.

'Never let me do anything like that again.'

'OK.'

'What you waiting for?' Adams gasped with sweat rolling down his face. 'Get in here and check out these horses.'

Tomahawk led both their horses into the darkness as his partner struck a match and started lighting every lamp he could locate.

It took only a matter of minutes for the old-timer to find the horse with the damaged shoe.

'This is it,' Tomahawk said triumphantly.

Gene Adams paced across to the creature as his friend led it away from the wall. His eyes looked at it for a while before he knew who had been riding it.

'This is Joshua Jones's mount,' he said, patting the creature's neck with his gloved hand. 'Scraggy old nag.'

'Reckon he's our man?'

Gene Adams pulled at his gloves until they were as tight as his very flesh. 'I reckon he's one of them.'

'Who's the other one?'

Adams said nothing as he patted the horse's neck thoughtfully.

Then both men heard the sound that

made the hairs on their necks stand on end.

It was the sound of a train whistle. The midnight train had arrived to be loaded with steers and passengers.

17

The two men from the Bar 10 rode hard down through the winding streets of McCoy heading for the railhead. Time was running out for them to find the thieves that they sought. This was becoming a race against time as they spurred their mounts through the darkness.

As they rounded the corner and headed down into the long stretch towards the railroad tracks, the shimmering lamps seemed to light up their galloping horses. The large black iron train stood tall and proud, taking on water from the tower as its crew busied themselves. The entire scene was almost unreal as dozens of men went about their duties in silent practised order. Only the hot smoke that bellowed from the tall train-stack gave the engine any real animation.

The stockpens were busy with wranglers cutting out the cattle for each of the high-sided wooden train carriages as Gene Adams and Tomahawk arrived on their lathered-up horses. They remained in their saddles watching the vast length of pens that faced the train. It was a scene of organized chaos that met their sore eyes.

Gene Adams watched with eyes that were narrowed and fixed. He was watching everything and everyone, trying to see the one man that he felt certain knew something of their missing gold: Joshua Jones.

His eyes focused upon the dozens of stock carriages that were coupled behind a single passenger carriage which in turn was behind the tender full of wooden logs all cut to the same length in order to fit inside the firebox of the engine. Clouds of steam poured out from vents at ground level as the train driver and his assistant adjusted the valves inside the open cab of the mighty locomotive.

Gene Adams gently spurred his chestnut mare forward and crossed over the railway tracks in front of the engine. Tomahawk followed on his gelding. Both riders moved along the length of the train on the quiet side, watching for anything out of place. The problem was that everything seemed to be correct.

'What we looking for, Gene?' Tomahawk asked as he cantered alongside his boss.

Here the darkness seemed comforting as the Bar 10 men moved alongside the train's length. Here they could move unobserved amid the shadows. Here they could watch without being watched.

At the end of the long train, a small guard's-van stood with its green and red lamps tacked upon its tail. Adams pulled his mare to a halt and stared at the scene of steers being loaded on to the numerous cattle trucks of the train. He had never been around when the train was loaded with his cattle before. He sold his steers and rode out before the train ever arrived. Seeing the dozens of men involved in the loading made him suddenly realize that their task was no simple one.

'What you thinking?' Tomahawk asked his friend.

'I got this feeling in my gut that we might have lost an awful lot of gold,' Gene Adams answered honestly. 'I'm starting to think that we've bitten off more than we can chew.'

'We'll get that Jones critter.'

'Maybe,' Adams heard himself say.

18

At five after eleven, Gene Adams and his friend Tomahawk watched from the sidewalk of the cattle agent's buildings as the last steers were loaded on to the train. Adams sat with his legs dangling over the edge of the boardwalk staring at his hunter pocket-watch before snapping the gold cover shut and placing it back in his coat pocket.

'What time is it now, Gene?' the old timer asked as he rose and stretched his legs.

'Just gone eleven,' Adams muttered. 'That train is leaving in an hour and we still haven't had a sniff of either Jones or our gold.'

Tomahawk was about to speak when his old eyes spotted a solitary man walking across the wide expanse of the cattle yards with a heavy saddle-bag slung over his shoulder. The figure walked like someone unused to using his feet. The high-heeled boots were made for fitting into the stirrups of a saddle, not for travelling any great distance on the ground. The hefty burden hanging over his shoulder made his task even tougher.

Gene Adams got to his feet, moved beside the bearded old man and gripped the small shoulders. 'What you reckon?'

'That's Joshua OK,' Tomahawk said, rubbing his hands together gleefully as he followed his boss down on to the dark dusty ground.

Adams and Tomahawk followed the man through the evening darkness towards the awaiting train. They soon gained on the slow-moving cowboy who was clearly struggling under the weight of the bags. They were like two hounds moving in on a stag.

Tomahawk moved wide as Adams headed straight for the man. The rancher caught up with Jones just as he reached the steps of the passenger cariage.

'What you got there, Mister Jones?' Adams asked in a deep curious tone.

Joshua Jones stopped and turned to face the man who stood with his gloved hands resting upon the handles of his golden forty-fives. The expression on the young cowboy's face seemed shocked at seeing his old boss. Shocked but not unduly worried.

'Mr Adams?' Jones seemed to be asking a question as he spoke the man's name. 'Is that you, Mr Adams?'

'Joshua.' Gene Adams moved into the lamplight and pushed his large hat back off his face. His black eyebrows hid his blue eyes as he tucked his coat back over the handles of his holstered guns. 'We've been looking for you.'

Jones glanced around the dark scene lit only by coal oil lanterns that hung from the train and railhead buildings. The sweat trickled down his face as he self-consciously touched the saddle-bag that hung over his left shoulder. 'What you mean, you been looking for me?'

Tomahawk moved into view causing the trail-hand to glance across at him. 'Howdy, Jones.'

'Tomahawk,' Jones stammered. 'What you doing here?'

'We got robbed.' Adams stepped closer to the nervous man. 'Some low-life stole our gold.'

Joshua Jones seemed unable to keep his feet still as he moved from one side to the next. His focus drifted from Tomahawk to Adams and back again. 'What the hell has that got to do with me, Mr Adams?'

'Maybe nothing at all.' Gene Adams pulled the leather of his gloves tight on his hands as he watched the scared man who stood just beneath the tall steps that led up into the safety of the train carriage.

Jones was about to turn and step up into the train when Adams' words burned into him.

'You ain't going anywhere, Joshua,' Adams said bluntly.

Jones lowered his leg back on to the ground and let go of the metal handrail. He stood staring at the lantern for several moments without looking at the two men who were steadily moving closer to him with every heartbeat.

'Undo that gunbelt, Jones,' Tomahawk advised the man, who was shaking from a combination of cold and fear.

Joshua Jones looked across at the old man. 'Stay where you are, Tomahawk. You as well, Adams. I ain't fooling.'

Tomahawk froze in his tracks and glanced over to Adams who was signalling for him to keep out of the action.

'You better back off, Adams,' Jones yelled as he carefully lowered the heavy saddle-bag to the ground. 'I ain't fooling.'

'Don't be a fool, Joshua,' Adams said in a fatherly voice. 'All we want is to look in that bag of yours.'

'What for?' Jones squared himself, holding the handle of his pistol tightly.

'You know why,' Adams told him.

The dozens of cattle trucks that made up the bulk of the long train started to echo to the sounds of beeves getting restless. The noises bounced off the buildings, sending chills down the spines of the three men. It was as if the steers knew that they were on their final journey and crying out to be spared.

'You reckon I'm a thief?' Jones snarled again.

'Maybe.' Gene Adams started to walk closer toward the man until a distance of only about twenty feet separated them.

'Stay back.' Jones seemed to shake from head to toe as he shouted at the rancher. 'I'll draw on you if you take one more step.'

Adams held his ground and tilted his head as he spoke to the restless man. 'If that's my gold in your bags you can get on the train and we won't do anything about it, Joshua. But you gotta leave the saddle-bags. If it ain't my gold just open up the bags and show us.'

Jones rubbed his sweating face anxiously. 'Think you're so big with those golden guns and that big ranch of yours, don't you?'

Adams stared at the shaking man. 'Take it easy.'

'Well I got something that I ain't letting go of.' Jones spat at the ground and kicked the bags to his side. 'You want them then you better be prepared to die in trying to get them.'

Tomahawk was starting to get worried as he watched both men squaring up to each other. He kept quiet for fear of distracting his boss.

'Well?' Jones started to slide his gun up and down in its holster as he edged toward the tall rancher. 'Draw, you yellow-livered skunk.'

Adams stepped backward from the man who approached him.

'I ain't gonna draw on you, boy,' he muttered.

'Coward,' Joshua Jones shouted, drawing his forty-five from its holster suddenly. 'Die!'

Gene Adams drew both his guns faster than the younger man and aimed them at him. 'Drop it.'

Joshua Jones seemed either unable or unwilling to listen as he continued to raise his gun toward Adams. Then the triggers were squeezed and confusion reigned.

The air was suddenly filled with the sound and sight of the exchange of gunplay. Jones had pulled his trigger before Adams but the man from the Bar 10 had returned the fire unwillingly.

Tomahawk ran towards the thick gunsmoke as Jones fell to the ground. As he crumpled into a heap, it was clear that he was dead.

Gene Adams stumbled backwards, dropping his guns as he fell.

The old-timer was quickly at his side. 'Gene. Gene . . . '

'I'm OK,' Adams said as he lay on his back.

'Then what's all this blood?' Toma-hawk ran his hand across the rancher's side. 'You're damn well leaking.'

Gene Adams accepted the help to his feet from the old man and opened his coat. 'He just winged me, Tomahawk. That's all.'

Tomahawk picked up his partner's guns and watched as the man walked towards the saddle-bags at the foot of the train steps.

'Open them up,' Adams ordered. 'Let's see why Jones thought it better to die than show us what was in here.'

Tomahawk unbuckled the bags revealing the golden coins.

'Well, this is half of the Bar 10 cattle money, Gene.'

Gene Adams slid his gold-plated guns into their holsters and watched as his friend lifted the bag off the ground.

'All we gotta do is find out who has the other saddle-bag, old friend,' Adams said through gritted teeth.

'We better get you to a doctor first.'

'Ain't got time.' Gene Adams stared at the watch in his gloved hand. 'We just ain't got enough time.'

19

Main Street was not the place that most doctors would choose to have an office let alone a home but Cyril Brewster was no normal doctor. Tomahawk ignored the revelries of McCoy's night life as he hammered his fists upon the doorway that led to a second floor office. The glass in the door shook as the old man continued to hit the framework. Gene Adams sat upon his chestnut mare watching his panicking partner making a fool of himself. He knew the wound was superficial and could sense that the blood had stopped seeping out of it. Yet Tomahawk continued to beat at the door with the gold lettering across it.

'Quit that, Tomahawk,' Adams said, holding the silver saddle horn. 'I don't need no quack.'

Tomahawk turned and pointed a finger and shook it. 'Maybe you are OK but what about Johnny back at Sutters Corner?'

Lamplight was suddenly visible coming from a window above them and then they could hear the very angry sound of a very angry voice as it descended the bare board stairs.

A man with white hair that was standing upright on his head walked up to the door and shouted through the glass.

'What in tarnation are you banging on my door for at this hour?' Doc Brewster yelled.

Tomahawk's jaw fell as he swung about to look at the man whose words steamed up the glass in the door. 'Eh . . . '

'What you want?' the doc shouted again, pulling up his black suspenders over his shoulders.

Gene Adams checked the saddle-bags that were tied firmly behind the cantle of his saddle before nodding at the strange old medical man. 'Tell him why you woke him up, Tomahawk.'

Tomahawk moved closer to the doorway and started to shout through the glass at the old doctor when a reflection caught his eye. He stared at the moving reflection for a moment before swinging around to watch the familiar chuckwagon as it gently rolled down the long street before heading out of town.

Gene Adams was staring at his open-mouthed friend so intently that he had not seen anything. 'What you gaping at?'

'The chuck wagon.' Tomahawk pointed down the dark street which glowed with orange lantern light.

Gene Adams turned in his saddle to gaze down the busy street.

'What chuck-wagon, Tomahawk?'

'Cookie's chuck-wagon, Gene.' The old-timer pointed.

'Where?' Adams squinted in vain.

'It turned at the end of the street.' Tomahawk was hopping up and down. 'I saw it. Honest.'

'You thinking what I'm thinking?'

Adams rubbed his chin as he began to wonder about the vicious-mouthed cook.

Tomahawk raised his white eyebrows. 'Worth checking on.'

Both cowboys gazed up at the doorway as they heard the key being turned in the lock and watched as the bare-footed old man stepped out on to the boardwalk.

'What do you boys want?' Doc Brewster shouted at them. 'You seem more interested in that old prairie ship than telling me what you want.'

'You saw the chuck-wagon too, Doc?' Gene Adams's face went suddenly serious as he looked down on to the old man.

'I might be old but unlike your hairy friend here, I ain't senile.' The doctor seemed to nod with every word as if hammering nails with his skull. 'Of course I seen it.'

Adams looked at his partner. The stare seemed to say everything between the old friends.

'Get mounted, Tomahawk,' he instructed.

As Tomahawk swiftly mounted his black gelding he gave the puzzled doctor a telling glare. 'Get dressed and ready for a long ride, Doc. We'll be back.'

Both Tomahawk and Gene Adams pulled their mounts away from the sidewalk and spurred. They galloped down the main street of McCoy and turned off on to the road out of town.

Riding into the blackness and along the trail that headed north, both riders stood in their stirrups taking the weight off their horses' backs. Adams's chestnut mare was snorting as she tried to gallop; the weight of the gold bullion in the saddle-bags was holding her back. It seemed longer but in reality it was only a matter of a few minutes before they caught sight of the wagon.

It stood across the dirt road in the moonlight with its lanterns lit and hanging from the secured tail gate. The four-horse team was motionless. It was too late for the riders of the Bar 10 to stop when rifle shots rang out from behind a boulder to their right amid a thicket of broad-leaf trees. The black gelding went down throwing its rider over his head into the dust. Gene Adams reined hard as he looked back at his friend lying in the middle of the trail like a discarded rag doll.

'Tomahawk!' he yelled as another shot rang out, passing by his face so close that he felt the bullet's heat. He quickly dismounted, leading the mare down into a deep gully off the dirt trail. Tying his horse to a tree he drew his left-hand forty-five and moved along the dark ditch towards the wagon.

As the gully got less deep he began to crouch, then crawl along using every blade of grass for cover. Holding his pistol firmly he peered over the edge of the gully, trying to see something. Anything.

It was so dark along this stretch of road out of McCoy that even the moonlight was unable to penetrate. The tall wide-leafed trees made it the perfect place for an ambush. Gathering his wits about him Adams knew roughly where the gunman must have been hiding when he fired upon them. Pulling back the hammer he fired six times in quick succession before holstering his empty gun.

Rifle shots were returned as fast as any Gene Adams had ever witnessed. They seemed to eat up the very edge of the gully above him. The smoke that drifted around in the dark midnight air gave the rancher the chance he had been seeking.

Adams ran for all he was worth and did not stop until he had reached the wagon. Resting behind the large rear wheel he drew out his right-hand Colt and moved along the familiar vehicle until he was standing beside the lead horse of the team.

Adams wished that it were lighter so he could see something out there besides his friend Tomahawk lying as still as death itself beside the dead black gelding.

'Give it up, Mr Adams.'

Adams's eyes widened as he heard the chilling voice bellowing around the scene of devastation. It was the familiar voice of Robert Bates. Or as he was better known, Cookie.

'Cookie?' the tall rancher shouted in response.

Answering the rifleman had been an error because now he knew where Adams was once again.

The bullets came in thick and fast from the dense undergrowth, sending the rancher rolling head over heels to avoid being hit. As Adams found himself upright again he fired several times. Then the ground beside him exploded as another rifle shot almost found its mark. Adams dragged himself across toward the shelter of a large tree when yet another bullet blasted its way into the trunk of the tree, sending burning sawdust and splinters into his face and eyes. His scream gave no indication of the true pain he suddenly felt. A pain like no other he had ever experienced in his long life.

Suddenly Gene Adams was lying with his back against the tree trunk fumbling for bullets from his gunbelt. Then the terrible realization struck him. He was blinded. Ripping off his bandanna he started to rub his burning eyes, trying desperately to clear the wood debris that was preventing him from seeing.

Another shot took the heel off his right boot and sent the rancher's heart beating even faster. He tried to reload his left hand Colt which he knew was empty but the burning pain made him drop the pistol. His hands could not find the weapon, so he sat for a few seconds beside the tree spitting on the bandanna, feverishly attempting to get the muck out of his eyes.

Then he heard the footsteps coming closer through the trees to his left. Dry twigs snapped under the weight of the approaching rifleman. The rancher felt a shudder rolling up his spine as his ears heard the man getting closer and closer.

'Mr Adams?' The chilling voice echoed inside Adams's head as he kept spitting on to the bandanna and rubbing the damp cloth along his burning eyelids. 'What's the matter, Mr Adams?'

Groping around at his side Adams found one of his forty-fives and tried to aim in the direction from which he could hear the footsteps.

Then, when he knew that the figure was too close for comfort, he squeezed the trigger. The hammer came down on a used cartridge and the sound of a simple click was all that filled the night air. Gene Adams quickly started to pull the trigger again and again until he finally realized that he had hold of his empty pistol. Before his hands could find the golden Colt with at least one bullet left he felt the cold steel of the Winchester touching his face.

'Get up, Mr Adams.' Cookie's voice

snarled into his head with the anger of a man who had consumed just the right amount of rye whiskey.

Somehow, Gene Adams fumbled his way on to his feet and kept trying to clear his eyes so that he could at least see his attacker.

'What's wrong?' Cookie laughed as he forced his rifle barrel into the man's side, making him stumble toward the chuck-wagon.

'I can't see,' Adams said pitifully as he limped along. The missing heel of his boot made walking in a straight line almost impossible except for the bruising thumps he got from Cookie's long rifle.

'Keep moving,' the voice coldly ordered him.

'Where are we going?' Adams asked as the rifle hit him hard in the back, causing him to fall on to one knee.

'To your horse,' Cookie replied, laughing with the laugh that only a man who was drunk on power ever used.

'You stole the gold with Jones, didn't

you?' Adams groaned as he managed to get back upright. 'A slick job.'

'So you found out about Jones?' Cookie gave another loud laugh. 'I told him to take the train.'

'He tried.' Adams grunted as he continued to be forced forward. His eyes at last started to clear but it was like looking through the bottom of a soda-pop bottle. Nothing was clear any more.

'You kill him?'

'Yep.'

'Good.'

'You sure are a loyal man to have on your side, Cookie.' Adams winced.

'So if you killed old Jones, that means you have the other half of the gold. Don't it?' Cookie grabbed Adams's shoulder and pulled him backward. 'I didn't wanna share it in the first place but old Josh was an awkward cuss.'

The tears streamed from Gene Adams's burning eyes as he gradually began to be able to focus once more.

'Yep. You're right, Cookie. Now you got the whole thing.'

'I deserve it. It was my idea,' Cookie laughed.

'It would have worked.'

'How did you find out about the switch so soon?'

'It was an accident.' Adams kept blinking feverishly.

'An accident, Mr Adams?' The angry rifleman laughed as he breathed into the rancher's face. 'Ain't that just the most annoying thing?'

Then suddenly, as they were directly in front of the chuck-wagon, Cookie forced Gene Adams down on to his knees. The cold steel of the Winchester barrel pushed into the nape of his neck as he heard the weapon being cranked slowly for the last time.

As if through a fog, Adams could see something that he thought was impossible. The skinny figure of his bearded friend standing next to the body of his dead horse in the middle of the trail road.

Cookie too saw the figure. 'Tomahawk?' he exclaimed.

Just as Adams felt the barrel of the carbine being raised from his neck to be aimed in the direction of the old-timer, he grabbed its cold length with all his might. His eyes might not have been working properly but his gloved hands still had their strength. Adams tugged the barrel down as he heard his friend shouting at the top of his lungs.

'Duck, Gene.'

The sound of the Indian stone axe as it cut its way from Tomahawk's hand through the air was unmistakable to Gene Adams's ears. He had heard it a thousand times over the years. The warning to duck was something he had never heard before but he did so just as the hatchet found its target.

Robert Bates fell backward as the axe hit him squarely in the head and slid over the wheel-rim into the dust.

Tomahawk stumbled to his friend's side and helped him to his feet.

'I thought you was a gonna,' Adams said.

'Disappointed?'

'Not hardly,' Adams chuckled. 'I forgot you were made of rubber.'

'Let me get some water for your eyes.' Tomahawk stepped over the body and pulled a canteen off the driver's seat. 'Cookie looks pretty dead to me.'

'That was a good shot,' Adams said as the old-timer gave him the canteen and he started to flush his pupils with the cold soothing liquid. 'Thank God you didn't try to use your gun.'

Tomahawk lifted up his axe and slid it into his belt.

'Weren't nothing.'

20

Sutters Corner had not been so busy in years as the buckboard pulled away from the hotel taking Doc Brewster back to McCoy. It had been a most profitable trip as he tended to young Johnny Puma's wounds and cleaned up Gene Adams's side and eyes. He had a pocket full of gold coins and the widest smile on his face that anyone had ever seen.

Gene Adams sat upon his chestnut and Tomahawk sat upon the pinto pony belonging to Johnny Puma. Old man Davis stood on the porch puffing on his corn pipe at the two cowboys.

'So old Tomahawk actually saved your bacon, Gene?' Davis laughed.

'That I did,' Tomahawk grinned, holding the reins tightly.

'He sure did,' Adams chuckled, patting his friend on the back.

Davis raised his pipe and saluted the old-timer with its stem across his forehead. 'A real hero.'

'That's the word I was looking for, Gene. Hero.' Tomahawk gave a jovial chuckle. 'That's me. Wait 'til I tells the boys back on the ranch.'

'We'll be back in two weeks' time, Davis.' Adams smiled at the hotelier. 'We gotta build my friend a statue.'

'Reckon that your Nancy can get our Johnny fit by then?' Tomahawk winked.

'I hope so.' Davis grinned. 'Doc Brewster said he's lost a heck of a lot of blood and has to rest until he makes it up.'

'Lots of rare steaks will do it.' Tomahawk's tongue seemed to emerge from the beard and trace his mouth.

'He'll get all the steak he can eat thanks to the money Gene gave me to look after the young 'un,' Davis puffed. 'I just hope my Nancy don't put a strain on him.'

'Oh to be young again,' Tomahawk

sighed with a wistful look on his craggy face.

'You were never that young, Tomahawk,' Gene Adams chuckled as he gathered his reins in his gloved hands.

The three men looked at each other for a moment with the regretful expressions upon their faces that only men with too many years under their belts have.

Gene Adams looked at the bulging bags tied firmly behind their saddles and thought about all the pain the gold had caused.

'Two weeks will give me enough time to break in a new saddle horse for myself.' Tomahawk scratched his whiskers. 'Then I can bring Johnny back this old pinto.'

Adams raised his arm as he pulled away from the hotel with Tomahawk following closely behind. The two horses trotted down the dusty trail that led towards the wide prairie. Davis watched as the two riders ambled away from his hotel with a smile upon his old face.

'Come on, Tomahawk. We gotta get back to the Bar 10.'

'I'm behind you. I'm right behind you.'

'*Adios amigo*,' Gene Adams called over his wide shoulder to Davis as he and his faithful friend headed for the trail that would take them home to the Bar 10 Ranch.

THE END

The stage robbery had been accomplished by an old woman. Twine Fourch had never heard of a female being a highway robber before. He followed the trail all the way to a dilapidated log cabin up Stone Mountain. What happened after that no one could believe even after townsmen from Jefferson found the old log house and the skeletal dying old woman. But before the mystery could be solved there would be two unnecessary killings, a bizarre suicide and a lynching.

GUNS OF THE GAMBLER

M. Duggan

Destitute gambler Ben Crow arrives in Mallory keen to claim his inheritance, only to discover that rancher Edward Bacon has other ideas. Set up by Miss Dorothy, who had fooled him completely, Ben finds himself dangling on the end of a rope. Saved from death, Ben sets off in pursuit of Miss Dorothy, determined upon retribution. However, his quest for vengeance turns into a rescue mission when she is kidnapped by a crazy man-burning bandit.

SIDEWINDER

John Dyson

All Flynn wants is to be Marshal of Tucson, but he is framed by the territory's richest rancher, Frank Buchanan, and thrown into Yuma prison. Five years later Flynn comes out, intent on clearing his name and burning for vengeance. Fists thud, knives flash and bullets fly as he rides both sides of the law and participates in kidnapping and double-dealing. He is once again arrested for a murder of which he is innocent. Can he escape the noose a second time?

THE BLOODING OF JETHRO

Frank Fields

When Jethro Smith's family is murdered by outlaws, vengeance is the one thing on his mind. He meets the brother of one of the murderers, who attempts to exploit Jethro's grudge in the pursuit of his own vendetta. The local preacher, formerly a sheriff, teaches Jethro how to use a gun. With his new-found skills, Jethro and his somewhat unwelcome friend pit themselves against seemingly impossible odds. Whatever the outcome lead would surely fly.

CRISIS IN CASTELLO COUNTY

D. A. Horncastle

The first thing Texas Ranger Sergeant Brad Saunders finds when he responds to an urgent call for help from the local sheriff is the corpse of the public prosecutor floating in the Nueces River. Soon Brad finds himself caught in the midst of a power struggle between a gang of tough western outlaws and a bunch of Italian gangsters, whose thirst for bloody revenge knows no bounds. Brad was going to have all his work cut out to end the bloody warfare — and stay alive!